tingle

OTHER BOOKS BY THE AUTHOR

Fiction:

Ladycat (as Nancy Greenwald)
The Girls and Me (as Nancy Alvarez)

Non-fiction:

Little Nancy, the Journey Home
(a memoir and workbook, as Nancy Alvarez)

BY NANCY ALVAREZ

Copyright © 2019 Nancy Alvarez

All rights reserved. No part of this publication may be reproduced, stored in a retrieval system, or transmitted by any means, electronic or mechanical, including photocopying, recording, or otherwise, except brief extracts for the purpose of review, without the written permission of the publisher.

This book is a work of fiction. Names, characters, places, and incidents are the product of the author's fevered imagination. Any resemblance to persons living or dead, to events, or to locales is entirely coincidental.

ISBN: 978-0-578-45654-6

Cover Design: Redwood Publishing / Chelsea L. Tompkins

Printed in the United States of America

For All My Women Friends

Acknowledgments

A special thanks to my publishing concierge, Redwood Publishing and Sara Stratton.

Chapter 1

Sara set down the vibrator her friend, Lucy, had urged her to buy, one shaped like a penis that could be filled with a viscous liquid if that was her pleasure. She felt close to tears: it wasn't what she wanted; it wasn't what she needed. She didn't want a plastic thing, as if that could satisfy. What she wanted was her husband, Jeffrey, his touch, his tongue, his scent, and the feel of him. She swung her feet over the side of the bed to the floor, and then sat there, just breathing. Would she ever get over missing her husband? He had tumbled over planting their tomatoes in the side yard of the condominium in the brownstone they shared with three other tenants over a year before, and she hadn't even noticed him lying there when she had come home from the market. By the time she had thought to wonder where he was and gone looking, there had been no point. Their family doctor

Nancy Alvarez

of many years had assured her it wouldn't have made any difference if she had found him an hour earlier. His death from the massive heart attack that felled him had been instantaneous. Doc McCaffrey would have told her the truth. The two couples had been playing scrabble together for years, Jeffrey by far the most creative player of the foursome. He had left her with a comfortable income between his pension and the social security she was able to collect; she didn't have to work. As she shimmied her jeans over her hips she wondered if that was actually helpful. If she had been forced to get out of the house and go to work she might have been less depressed.

As she plugged in her espresso maker, she wondered if she should look in the paper for a part-time job, or even ask some of her friends and neighbors if they had heard of anything she might find interesting. After all, she knew she was still attractive even though she had cut off her long, auburn tresses months ago because she thought she looked perkier in the bob the stylist had suggested. It fell to her chin line, and waved back and forth when she walked. She rarely thought about how she looked anymore. Why bother?

She sat down with a sigh, her latte, the latte Jeffrey had insisted she learn how to make – "After all, I might not be here forever" he had teased – on the table before her. Neither of them imagined that at fifty-two he wouldn't be making her lattes for many years to come. Or that she might not be there to drink them. She was only 44. On the bright side, she wouldn't be sitting down to drink the marvelous coffee concoction he had been making for years if he hadn't pestered her into learning how to make it too. Her homemade latte was actually better than the one she sometimes bought from the local barista on Greenwich Avenue when she was in a hurry. The piece of toast she had made to go with her morning brew was hard to swallow, even with butter. Everything tasted like cardboard to her and had for so long she had forgotten what it felt like to enjoy a good meal at home or in a restaurant. One of her friends had managed to coax her to a neighborhood bistro by making a reservation and walking over to pick her up. That meal she had actually enjoyed, but afterwards everything returned to bland.

She looked for the book she had been reading, realizing she had finished it the preceding afternoon, the last novel in a stack she had gotten at 'Three Lives & Company' only a week before. Maybe she would walk over to the Jefferson Market Library after she had washed her few dishes and laid them on a towel on the counter to dry. She never accumulated enough dishes for the dishwasher, and rarely used it anymore. She could even take a walk through Washington Square Park afterwards – a novel idea – leaving the new books she had chosen with Michael, the librarian there who had been suggesting books to her for several years. She was surprised to realize she hadn't been to the library in months. Maybe he had found another job. She was startled to realize she would miss him if he had.

She stuck her head out of the sliding doors leading to their patio, noticing the empty planter boxes where Jeffrey had always planted lettuce, carrots, and peas on the lattice-work panel he had lugged home from a nursery in Chelsea a few years before. It still looked serviceable to her as she grabbed a sweater from the tree rack in the hallway by the front door. Maybe she'd buy some fall plants at the nursery on the way home as a way to honor Jeffrey. The air was crisp and clear, the sky above blue as only the sky could be on such a day in New York City. She sighed. It was good that she was forcing herself to go to the library.

Michael was surprised to see Sara come into the foyer. She was one of his favorite regulars, and he had been wondering just the other day if something had happened to her. She was in her early forties, he thought, so he had doubted she was ill, or worse.

"Well hi, stranger," he called out before she turned to climb the stairs to the adult reading room. Sara took a detour to walk over to the reference desk where he was standing. Usually ebullient, she stood there mute.

"Are you OK?" he asked, his liquid brown eyes crinkling with concern at the corners. They were a lighter shade than his skin, which always glowed, as if he lathered himself with oil before donning his clothes. She was sure he didn't, and it was just the texture of his skin.

At first Sara didn't reply and then she mumbled, "My husband died," faltering because she didn't know how to continue.

"How old was he?" the librarian blurted before he could stop himself. He really was shocked. He was sure she was younger than he was.

Sara sighed. "Fifty-two," adding irrelevantly "It was completely unexpected."

"I am so sorry," he said, and he was. He had also chosen books for her husband, though not as frequently. He had seemed like a very decent guy.

She sighed. "Yes, so am I."

"Reading helps?" he asked.

She shook her head in response, adding, "I can escape in novels."

"Then let's find you some good ones," he suggested, motioning to the boy who was stacking returned books on the rolling cart behind the desk. "I won't be gone long," he told him, adding, "Do you remember how to check someone out?"

"Yes, I'll be fine," the boy assured Michael, who stepped out from behind the counter to walk upstairs to the fiction shelves with Sara.

Tingle

After he had grabbed a new mystery by Faye Kellerman and another by Michael Connolly, he rested his hand on her upper arm, sending an electric current all the way up to his shoulder, which certainly came as a shock. It was totally inappropriate given the circumstances. "Is there anything else I can do?" he asked anyway, persevering.

When Michael's hand had momentarily rested on her arm, Sara had felt a pins-and-needles sensation, as surprised by the response as Michael had been by his. 'At least I'm not dead too' she thought irreverently, managing to cover her shock. She sighed again, although before Jeffrey's death sighing had not been part of her repertoire. "This helps," she finally replied, lifting up the books she was now holding in her arms.

"Would you like to get a glass of wine later?" he asked, totally surprising himself for the second time in minutes. When he saw the startled look on her face, almost like an animal caught in the headlights, he added, "Or we could just go to the coffee shop on the corner when I get off at 4:00."

By then she had composed herself, realizing she wanted to accept the invitation. She had only been 'out' with her women friends, and the thought of spending a half hour with someone of the opposite sex was actually appealing. "Wine sounds better than coffee," she smiled. "I'm not sleeping very well, so caffeine after 5 is probably not a good idea."

His smile was as warm as his eyes. "I'd prefer wine anyway, but I didn't want to presume."

Laughing, she said, "You already have, thank God." She couldn't believe anyone's smile could be so wide, spreading from ear to ear, or that's how it seemed. "What time should I come back?"

"4:15 would be safe. Then we can walk over to Amelie together."

Nancy Alvarez

When she let herself back into her condo, Sara decided to read in bed. Maybe she'd be able to take a nap so the wine wouldn't make her nod off later; she had plenty of time. She always had plenty of time. Still, sleep was not in the offing; she kept remembering the feel of his hand on her arm.

Another sigh, and then she opened the Kellerman, knowing she'd enjoy reading about Rina and Decker, even if she couldn't keep track of the unfolding mystery. Focus had been as big a problem as sleep these past, slow, endless months. She did drop off with the book on her chest, waking with a start and realizing it was already 3. She jumped up, shucking her clothes as she headed for the bathroom to take a quick shower, hoping it would revive her. Afternoon naps, when she did take them, always left her feeling dopey. By 4:05 she was already standing outside the library, breathless because she had jogged there from her condo. She had thought it would take her longer to reach West 10th Street, and took several deep breaths to calm herself down. Why in the world was she so nervous?

Inside, Michael was again looking at his watch, which he had been doing since Sara had left the library with four books, not just the original two. Even going on a first date had never made him feel so discombobulated. It felt ridiculous.

When he walked outside and saw her standing below him at the bottom of the steps, the feeling vanished. He realized he liked this woman and felt compassion for her loss.

There was a chill in the air, so they picked up their pace and were at the wine bar within minutes. Along the way they chatted about nonsense, both assuming their conversation would improve once they had each had a few sips of the Bordeaux Michael suggested ordering as soon as they sat down.

Tingle

"What do you read when you're not at work," she asked him as soon as the waiter had uncorked the bottle and left them to their own devises.

"I actually prefer nonfiction to fiction," he admitted. "Except for James Baldwin, who I can read over and over again, especially 'The Fire Next Time'."

"Me too," she agreed, "Though you already know that. What kind of nonfiction? What subjects?"

"Michael Eric Dyson. Noam Chomsky," he began, surprising her.

"My husband studied under Chomsky at MIT and read everything he published thereafter. He went to seminars at his house when he was a student. I think he wished he could have stayed in Boston, but work beckoned."

"When did he meet you?" Michael asked.

"His third year as a grad student at MIT. At the MIT library," she quipped. 'Just kidding.'

Again that marvelous smile.

"I've never been married, though I did have one committed relationship for a few years. It ended over a year ago," he added. He had never opened up with anyone easily, but it suddenly seemed the most natural thing in the world to be telling Sara this fact.

"Why did you break up? Or did she break up with you?" Sara asked, immediately apologizing for being intrusive.

"You're not," he assured her, surprised that her questions didn't bother him. "We never even lived together, but she broke up with me because I didn't want to get married."

At that Sara raised her eyebrows.

"I told her it was because I don't believe in marriage, and even though that's true I don't think that was an honest answer." He paused and Sara waited for him to continue, instinctively knowing that was the right thing to do. "I don't think I loved her," he finally said in a near-whisper. "God, why did I see her for so long?" he asked, obviously a rhetorical question since Sara certainly wouldn't know the answer.

"My mother was married to my father who deserted her when I was one," Michael began. Again Sara remained silent. "I met him once when she took me to the apartment where he was crashing a few blocks from ours." Again he paused. "He patted me on the head but didn't ask me one question about my life. It was worse than if I hadn't seen him, and she knew." A longer pause. "My mother is great. She wouldn't have been happier married to him, but she might have if she had married someone else…."

"Have you ever asked her why she didn't?" Sara wanted to know. "You don't have to answer."

Michael looked startled. "I've never thought of doing that," he mused.

"You could," Sara suggested gently.

"What if it brings it all back and makes her unhappy?" he asked in turn.

"That wouldn't last forever, and it might open a new avenue of communication between the two of you," she replied.

"We're actually pretty close," he told her.

"It doesn't mean you won't still be close," she said, pouring them each another glass of the burgundy.

"I've never even thought about this, at least not for years, and here I am talking to a virtual stranger about it," he muttered.

Sara tried to lighten the mood. "I'm not a stranger. You know every book I've read in the last couple of years because you suggested each and every one of them to me," she teased. She reached across the table, moving the wine bottle so she could, and laid her hand gently atop his. They both stared at one another, no longer able to hide the effect touching seemed to have on each of them.

"I'm really not ready for a relationship," he explained.

"Neither am I," she agreed.

"And yet here we are," he sighed.

"Yes."

"We could try meeting for wine once a week as friends," she suggested. Michael looked visibly relieved, although her hand was still resting upon his own.

"I would like that very much," he said, and then rose to pay the bill. When they parted in front of the wine bar he leaned over and kissed the top of her head, turning and heading back up Sixth Avenue without looking back.

On the one hand Sara was relieved that she found his touch exciting. She had doubted she would ever feel a sexual thrill again, even though she was only 44. On the other hand she had no idea what to do about it, or if she wanted to do anything at all. Would Jeffrey see any further involvement with the librarian as a betrayal of the years they had shared? That was silly she thought as she unlocked her front door. He wouldn't know, and even if he did, he wouldn't have wanted her to stop living. Which, really, was what she had been doing. Perhaps the rush she had just experienced merely indicated she was coming back to life and didn't have much to do with the librarian himself.

He was just so damned attractive. How come she had never noticed that before? She could have noticed but not felt the charge, but she hadn't. Sara decided to run a bath, a very hot one since cold was totally unappealing given the autumn chill in the air outside.

Maybe hot water, if she made it hot enough, would have the same effect as cold on her revived libido.

She made it so hot she couldn't even put her whole foot in the tub, jerking it out as soon as it touched the water. She began again, with just her toes: body part by body part she lowered herself into the tub.

It seemed that hot water had the opposite effect from the one she desired. She kept picturing his hand beneath hers, the length of his fingers with the neatly trimmed nails, pink against his brown skin. Good Lord. Maybe she should start going to the library on 23rd Street, the Muhlenberg. At least that was what she thought it was called. The notion of not seeing Michael again was as distressing as seeing him. As she dried herself on the pale blue bath sheet that hung beside the tub, she decided she would revisit the problem the following day.

On Wednesday Sara met her women friends for their monthly dinner get-together. She had made a yogurt chicken dish for their potluck, grasping it with potholders as she carried it over to her friend's apartment a few blocks from her own. She looked forward to these monthly get-togethers, which Marty had initiated because she had obviously been worried about her friend's state of mind since Jeffrey's death. Marty had been right, and the potlucks had definitely improved her spirits.

Once they were all seated around Marty's large, round, wooden oak table, a throw-back to the 70's when the claw foot tables were selling like hotcakes at the local 'antique' shops, Marty asked if anyone had anything new to report.

"Actually, I do," Sara said hesitantly. She wasn't sure she wanted to talk about Michael, but her feelings were new, and she realized, important to share.

Tingle

"I know some of you go to our lovely local library as much as I do," she began, heart beating. "So you probably know who Michael is…"

"The gorgeous black guy who mans the front desk," Elaine declared with a grin. "Yum!"

"Oh stop it," Sara laughed, "But yes, that Michael."

"And…" Marty urged.

"Well, a few nights ago we went out for a glass of coffee…well, actually wine, when he got off work," Sara said, hurrying on before anyone could interrupt with a salacious comment. "It was nothing. I mean, it was very enjoyable, but not what you think."

"I know what I'd be thinking," Marty groaned.

"Hahaha," Sara said. "I really had a great time. He's smart and funny…"

"And gorgeous," Lucy took her turn to tease.

"Yes, he's gorgeous too," Sara concurred.

"Come on," Marty begged. "Get to the dirt."

"If you keep pushing, I won't say another word," Sara cautioned.

"Shut up, Marty. I want to hear the whole story," Elaine commanded.

The other women waited for Sara to continue. She was looking at her feet, which only proved there was more to the story. Finally Sue, who was the quietest member of the group, broke her silence. "Come on! Even I want to hear more!" which made them all laugh.

Looking up Sara mumbled, "When we were getting up to leave, he put his hand on my back to lead me out the door."

"Oh my!" from Lucy. She sighed loudly, causing more laughter.

"Come on you guys. Shut up," Sue demanded.

Again they all waited.

"Do not make a big deal out of this or I won't meet you all next month," said Sara, pausing. Her friends knew enough to keep quiet. "I felt a tingle," Sara sighed.

"I feel a tingle just looking at him," Lucy blurted, unable to stop herself.

"Yeah, well, wait till he puts a hand on your back," Sara groused.

"Actually that's a good thing, isn't it," Marty proposed. "Now you know that you're still alive."

"Yes! That's just what I decided," Sara agreed. "I'm still alive!"

"You do know that Jeffrey would be cheering the loudest," Lucy suggested gently, no longer making a joke of the whole event.

"Do you think?" asked Sara, relieved when every one of her friends agreed this was so. "I don't think it's a big deal," she began, but all of them interrupted with "Yes it is. It is so. Of course it is."

None of them thought it was too soon to do something proactive about the librarian, although Sara did. Nonetheless, it was a relief to know none of them thought it was shameful – did she really think that? All of her friends agreed it was actually a positive sign.

When they had parted at the entrance to Marty's building and Sara was again walking home with her casserole dish, she felt relieved. But she also promised herself she wouldn't do a thing about what she felt around him, and would certainly not say anything to Michael. Friendship was fine, but that was it.

. . . .

Michael was even more disturbed than Sara by the shock that had coursed through him when he had touched her back. It wasn't merely that he hadn't felt anything close to that with his last girlfriend, but that he had felt something so powerful with a white woman. He had only dated black women, having decided that explaining his background, his mother, and his upbringing would just have been too damned difficult with someone who was white. A black woman would have similar stories and at the very least understand his. Of course he also hadn't shared much of anything with the women he had dated, not just the last one. At an early age he had learned that most women put up with a lot if you were thoughtful, kind, and asked questions about them and their lives. Most of the women he had dated had known he earned a decent living at the library, which added to his acceptability. That he was good looking couldn't have hurt, though he rarely thought about that. His face was just part of who he was.

By the time he put his key in the lock and opened the front door to his compact one-bedroom apartment a block from the Hudson River, he had decided that he could still meet Sara for wine because he enjoyed her company, but more than that was out of the question. If it became an issue, he would find some way to explain his feelings about who he could and could not date, although he did wish she was less attractive. When she had started to cry as she talked about Jeffrey's death, there had been no way for him to ignore the green of her eyes or the tenderness he had felt for her. Her new haircut looked great, but he hadn't said anything about that for obvious reasons. He had held himself back, although he had longed to stand up, take her in his arms, and hold her in an effort to help staunch her tears. He knew enough to resist.

Neither of them needed more grief in their lives.

Chapter 2

When he didn't see her for several weeks, Michael was surprised by how disappointed he felt. Sara avoided the library for more than three weeks, but by then she had finished the Kellerman book as well as the Connolly. She didn't like reading on her computer because she liked to lie on the couch to read, and though she tried, she knew reading on line was not the solution. Only Lucy knew about her addiction to mysteries, and didn't seem to think there was anything wrong with it. Neither did Michael, for that matter, who had recommended a few new authors to her over the past year. Robert Crais had been her favorite. If figuring out the intricate plots took her mind off her own losses, she should take out as many mysteries as she could carry home. At least that's what Lucy told her. It was Sara who blamed herself for indulging in such an anti-intellectual pursuit.

Nancy Alvarez

When she entered the lobby of the library behind an older man who held the door for her so she could pass through, Sara was relieved to see that Michael was not behind the desk. She would not admit she also felt disappointed, and squelched the thought by walking quickly upstairs to the fiction stacks and browsing the 'new' arrivals. She quickly became engrossed with her search, pulling out first one book to read the plot description and then another. When she felt a hand on her shoulder she almost jumped half a mile.

"I wondered if you'd ever come back," he said with a very warm smile, though not the wide grin she'd begun to associate with him.

Sara shrugged. "I thought of going to 42nd Street," she admitted, "but that seemed sort of silly." She wished he'd take his hand away from her shoulder.

"I'm glad you didn't do that," Michael said quietly. "There's no reason we can't be friends, even good ones."

Her sigh was so huge it even raised her shoulders.

"Is it because..." Michael began, but she interrupted.

"No! Of course not!" She felt herself blushing as she explained, "I dated a guy from Ghana when I was in college, before I met Jeffrey and he swept me off my feet." When he didn't respond immediately, she added, "God that sounds awful. Kind of like 'some of my best friends'...she trailed off and then looked up at him. His eyes were looking at her with so much warmth she wanted to crawl inside them, but of course refrained.

"I've actually never dated a white woman," he agreed. When he saw her discomfort he added, "But that's not what we would be doing anyway."

Before she could stop herself, Sara suggested, "We could meet for a glass of wine again today or tomorrow when you get off work."

Tingle

Then he smiled the smile she loved. "As friends," he quipped.

She smiled back at him. "Yes, as friends." Sara really liked this man, and realized how often she had talked to him over the past years, about books, a headline in the Times, the snow and whether it would stick – meaningless stuff. She had even mentioned the librarian to Jeffrey, who said he sometimes talked to him too. Both of them had always loved libraries, even as children. But now Jeffrey wasn't there anymore and everything felt different.

What would Jeffrey have done? Protected her? He wouldn't have needed to because Sara never noticed other men once they were together, except in passing. He had been more than enough for her.

"How about tomorrow?" Michael interrupted her thoughts. "I'm meeting my personal trainer at the gym today."

"Ahhh. That explains it," she laughed.

Michael looked down at his flat belly. "It's embarrassing that I care about that, but I do," he admitted, which made her laugh aloud, suppressing the sound because of where they were standing. Several other patrons were perusing the fiction stacks. In whispers they agreed to meet at the same wine bar the next day at 4:30.

Each of them was disappointed that they weren't meeting at 'their place' right then, but neither voiced those feelings aloud. Michael was relieved he had books to sort and customers to help the rest of the day because otherwise he would have been anxious about the following afternoon, which was still ridiculous. Later Michael's trainer had to grab the weight bar as Michael was raising it above his head because it was obvious his mind was elsewhere. "Whoa, Mike. Take it easy. You're someplace in outer space." No one else called him Mike. He didn't think he was a Mike, but had never corrected the kid.

Nancy Alvarez

When he had changed into sweats at his apartment and collapsed into his favorite chair, he took a sip of the Laphroaig he had poured as soon as he had come inside. He rarely drank during the week, but when he did he drank the good stuff. He didn't refrain from pouring a second shot.

He knew he wanted more with Sara than mere friendship, no matter how unwise that might be. He felt a shiver in his bones from just looking into her eyes; he didn't even have to be touching her. He went into the kitchen to chop vegetables for his dinner, hoping that activity would replace the image of the swell of Sara's breasts in the blue silk blouse she had been wearing in the library. He had almost gasped when she unbuttoned the sweater she was wearing over it as she turned to talk to him by the fiction stacks.

After Sara ate her dinner, reheated orange chicken with quinoa and a salad, she grabbed some three-by-five cards and sat down at her dining room table. She began noting topics she and Michael could talk about the following day, something she hadn't done since high school, preparing for her first few awkward dates.

"And this isn't a date," she reminded herself. Nevertheless, she continued to jot down subjects that seemed 'safe' to her. "I don't know if I want to be safe,' she thought, totally nonplussed. Jeffrey hadn't been the only man she had slept with, but had certainly been the only one over the past twenty years. She had noticed other men – after all, she wasn't comatose – but that was all. Her marriage had been all consuming. The notion that she might want to make love to someone else, might actually make love to someone else now, was frightening. She thought of calling Lucy, but didn't pick up the phone. Lucy probably would have urged her to enjoy what was happening, and not worry about being 'safe'. It was time for her to explore areas that might not feel comfortable, her friend would have urged, more power to her. After all, she was only in her early forties.

Sara was startled when she remembered that Jeffrey had teased her about 'her friend the librarian' a few times, but both had known it was a tease and nothing more. Neither had given it serious thought.

Sara poured herself a large glass of the red wine she had been saving for a special occasion.

Meeting Michael the following day was different. It wasn't anything to joke about. What was she getting herself into? She suspected her little note cards would not save her. From what, she didn't want to think about anymore.

It turned out that Sara didn't need her little three-by-five cards. Before they had even sat down, Michael was telling her about a particularly annoying library patron who had asked for help finding fiction he might like, but then dismissed every single author Michael suggested. He had either read all the books by that author, or had only read one, which he hadn't liked at all. When Michael pointed to the new fiction rack, the man got up, incensed. "That's your job, to help me!" he had declared loudly enough that several people standing nearby had turned to see what was going on. "I'm sure you'll find something you'll like in our new fiction selections," Michael had calmly replied, or so he told Sara.

"Do you have to deal with many people like him?" Sara asked with some surprise, adding, "You always made great suggestions to me."

"I liked you," he replied, grinning. "That guy is almost always a pain in the ass. But no, I don't get many like him, thank God."

Without thinking it through, he reached out and grabbed her hand, squeezing gently. Then he sat there holding it, wondering why he had done that. He wouldn't have grabbed the hand of any of his other female friends, although he didn't have many of those he realized with a start. He let go as quickly and gently as he could and asked her about her week to cover his discomfort.

They shared life stories for almost two hours, until Sara was so hungry she said, "I'm starving. For now, we have to stop, but we can do this again next week, same time, same place."

"Why don't we grab a bite before we each head home," he suggested.

"I can't. I already have a roast in my crockpot, and if I don't get home, it'll be totally charred," she replied.

"I thought crockpots slow-cook everything," he said, surprised.

"They do, but you can't leave something in there for more than 8 hours without it getting overcooked, even on low," she explained.

"OK," he agreed. He held her jacket and helped her into it. The weather had cooled almost overnight, and each had grabbed one when they had left their apartments earlier. Again he put his hand on her back to guide her out the door of the little wine bar. Again, each felt a jolt. Again, each silently vowed to avoid physical contact the next time they met.

On his way home Michael reminded himself that he didn't think he was ready for any romantic relationship, let alone one with a white woman. He needed to figure out why he had felt so much distance from his last 'significant other', and why he had never lived with any of the women that had been in his life. Was he really such a private person? He didn't talk very openly to his few close male friends either, at least about deeply personal subjects. None of them talked to him that way either, though two had been his friends since college.

Tingle

Although she had finished the books she had taken out of the library by the end of the weekend, long before their next wine venture, Sara again avoided the library. Since the idea of not having anything to read was unbearable, she broke down and ordered a book on her computer, which reminded her how much she hated to read at her desk. Reading was a way to unwind, to relax: sitting at her desk staring at her computer screen as she read page after page of the novel was horrible. Nonetheless she still waited to walk over to Amelie until the day of the scheduled meeting.

Michael arrived at the wine bar by 4:05, having grabbed his jacket fifteen minutes before he had to leave. When the woman who took his place behind the desk every Tuesday arrived, he was ready to walk out the door. Since this was unusual she quipped, "You must have one hot date!" Shrugging, he laughed. Had his skin been able to turn pink she would have noticed his blush. He certainly felt it, and hurried from the desk.

Sara arrived a few minutes later, early as well. Again they talked for a few hours, and again Sara had something cooking in the crockpot, chicken with vegies this time.

"Maybe you should get chopped meat next week, so you can make your burgers whenever you get home," he teased. Then he thought to ask, "They don't get cooked in that thing too, do they?"

She shook her head 'no' as she shrugged her arms into the sleeves of her jacket. As they reached the door, she turned to add something. He leaned over and brushed her lips with his as she stood in the doorway. Then he closed the door behind them, speechless. He couldn't say 'I don't know why I did that' because he did. He had wanted to kiss her the first time they had come to the small bar for their first glass of wine. Since she was still facing him, he leaned in and kissed her again, this time with more force. Her mouth opened, her tongue tickling his. They didn't pull apart until another patron cleared his throat so he could enter the wine bar.

"I'll see you next week, when I return the books I got today," she blurted and turned quickly to walk away. Michael didn't try to stop her, staring after her until she turned the corner on 11th Street.

'Why did I do that' he asked himself. 'She kissed me back,' he marveled. Then, 'Why did I wait so long to kiss her?' and finally, 'Now what?'

'Now what?' were also the words whirling around in Sara's head as she turned the corner. She was both shocked by how brazen she had been, and elated. Kissing him had felt marvelous. She forced herself to eat the chicken that had been cooking in the crockpot, putting most of it in a glass container, and then sitting down on her couch. By nine she decided to repair to the bed she had shared with Jeffrey because she had been unable to read one word of the Paretsky mystery she had chosen to read first. Since she couldn't concentrate on the new Sue Grafton either, she turned out the light and tossed and turned until two in the morning.

When she couldn't stand it any longer, she grabbed her laptop and looked Michael up in the white pages. There he was, phone number and all. With shaking hand, she dialed his number. If he wasn't awake too, he would be soon. After he said 'hello' not sounding the least bit groggy, she said, "We have to talk," without even bothering to identify herself.

"When?" he asked, fully alert.

Sara hadn't awakened him; he had been lying in bed for hours too. Hearing his voice felt quite soothing. It sounded in her ear again because she hadn't responded. "What's your address?" he asked. She gave him the address without hesitating, and her apartment number so she could buzz him into the brownstone, and then took out a bottle of champagne that had been chilling in her refrigerator for months. She couldn't even remember which of her friends had given it to her, knowing how much she loved the stuff. She then raced into her bedroom, stripped the bed, and put on her favorite set of Bed & Bath sheets, blue and lavender stripes. She hoped Michael liked the colors.

He must have jogged all the way from his apartment to hers, arriving within minutes, just as she was putting the champagne bottle into an ice bucket in her living room. Now that she had someone to share it with, uncorking it seemed a good idea. When she heard the bell sound from the lobby, she was startled, and glanced at her watch. Wow. Barely ten minutes had passed since they had hung up. She crossed to the hallway and buzzed him upstairs.

When she opened the door, they fell into each other's arms. She could barely get the door closed as they kissed and kissed. Clearly neither of them was wondering what they were doing anymore. Or if they were, they had decided to do what came naturally and stop agonizing about it.

'My God he's a good kisser,' she thought as she took his hand to lead him to her bedroom.

He took her face in his long, slender fingers, holding her still so she had to look into his eyes. "Are you sure?" he asked, no smile now, totally serious.

Swallowing, she nodded 'yes'. But when they reached the bedroom she had shared with Jeffrey, she stopped.

"Your husband?" he whispered, understanding even before she did.

"Do you mind if we use the guestroom?" she asked him, reaching for his hand to lead him there. "I even changed the sheets on my bed, but the ones in here are fresh too, just not my favorites...."

"What color are your favorites?" he asked, smiling and stroking her hair.

"Blue and lavender," she replied, surprised she could still speak.

"Good colors," he agreed. "Perhaps we can use them next time."

There would be a next time, she thought joyously. She had never had a one-night stand, even before Jeffrey.

"I've never been a guy for one-night stands," he murmured, as if he could read her thoughts. Her delighted smile made him smile as well. Together they could have lit up the entire hallway.

She was so nervous she could barely unbutton her blouse while he easily pulled his jersey over his head. Without pausing he reached down, covering her hand with his and easily completed the process of unbuttoning, gasping at the lacy black bra she was wearing beneath the blouse. Then he lowered the bra down her arms, which made Sara groan aloud. When he gently licked first one nipple and then the other, she thought she would pass out. Instead she reached down and unbuckled his belt, and then unzipped his black pants. This time it was Michael who groaned.

"I haven't felt this way in years," he murmured.

"Me neither. Not for a very long time." She said no more. Talking about the sex life in her marriage seemed rather unsuitable, she thought, and then his very erect penis popped out of the opening she had created.

"Oh my," she giggled. "What they say about black men is true!"

He roared with laughter. "Don't know. I've never seen the erect cock of any of my friends." Which made them both laugh, slowing their progress.

Then he bent to her nipples again, taking first one and then the other fully into his mouth. He rolled each soft breast in his hands, continuing to brush the nipples with his mouth.

Tingle

"We have to lie down," she managed to murmur, and then they fell on her guestroom bed.

He said, "We should take our time," although he continued what he had started when they were on their feet. She was already pulling his pants down around his ankles, and then his thigh-length boxers.

"Buck naked," he groaned, though he still wore his socks.

"Soon," she replied, stroking his balls.

"Your turn," said Michael. First he removed her underpants from beneath her skirt. She had forgotten that was what she had thrown on before she found the champagne and changed her sheets. The sheets they weren't lying on. Then he unzipped the skirt, and carefully pulled it over her hips and down.

When he buried his face in the thick auburn hair of her pussy she screamed, "Oh my God,", or that's what it sounded like to her: embarrassingly loud.

"God has nothing to do with this," he disagreed. "Though if there is such a thing, he or she should."

Given what he was doing with his tongue, she couldn't have possibly replied. "Oh please, oh please," she eventually begged, though she had already come once. What she was asking him for she had no idea. She did wonder if he had always gotten this hard with his past girlfriends. When he rolled on top of her, she said, "Uh uh. Your turn now!" and kneeled above him.

His penis seemed huge, though she couldn't picture Jeffrey's. She thought he had been smaller, and then the thought was gone. Her deceased husband did not belong in this bed with them. She tried to say, "Don't stop breathing," but the words weren't intelligible because her mouth was filled with him.

Then she moved up the shaft, tickling his cock all the way up to the tip with her tongue. She licked the tip, around and around, until he grabbed her hair and pulled her back up.

"You have to stop or I'll come."

Still on her knees she grinned broadly. "I thought that was the idea"

He reached for her, whispering, "The first time I come with you, I want to be inside."

"And the second time?" she teased, but he had already pulled her down across the length and breadth of him, and was sliding inside her. She must have been very wet for him to be able to do that with her on top of him.

"Oh Jesus," he managed to sputter and then he exploded.

"Wow" she said, and then added, "Neither Jesus nor his father have anything to do with this," she teased, "or so you said." Then she asked, "How long do you think it will take you to come again?"

"I have no idea," he answered. "I might not be able to."

"Well, let's see," she murmured as she again took his penis into her mouth.

"You don't have to do this," he groaned, the distress on his face apparent.

"But I want to," she replied as best she could, given that he was again growing in her mouth. "You taste salty, and kind of tangy," she added with some amazement. He cried out when he came, looking quite shocked at how quickly she had brought him to a second climax.

"As you said before, the son of God has nothing to do with this," she giggled while swallowing.

"God, you don't have to do that either."

"I bet it's protein," she laughed, and stopped abruptly when she realized he had parted her legs, his tongue easily homing in on her clitoris. He was circling it with his tongue. Her legs began to shake so badly she couldn't control them.

"Let go," he murmured as he continued what he had begun.

He was flicking his tongue around the entire area as he spread her lips open with his long fingers, baring her button and relishing the shaking of her body. When she came it was with shuddering gasps "Oh God Oh God Oh God!"

"Do you always hold your breath when you come," he teased.

"I don't remember," she replied, and then relaxed with a sigh. "Oh God!"

He then said with a gentleness that amazed her, "You can cry if you need to. I almost did."

As tears dribbled down her chin she asked, "Why didn't you?"

"It wouldn't have been manly," he answered, unsmiling.

"Are you serious?" she asked, rising up on her elbows to look into his eyes.

"Kind of," he shrugged.

She laid her hand on his penis and said, "I don't think you have to worry about that at all."

For several moments they lay side by side without speaking in Sara's guestroom bed.

Then Michael said, with some hesitation, "We're going to keep doing this, aren't we?"

"Oh yes!" she exclaimed, and then blushed with embarrassment.

"At least I can see it when you blush," he murmured, to bring some levity into what was happening between them. His arms went around her, and he sighed with contentment. Then he asked, "Can I still recommend books to you?"

They both began to laugh until Michael stopped, and then Sara's giggles renewed his own, and so it went.

Both of them slept the sleep of the dead the rest of the night. He was almost late for work, which she wondered about as she fixed herself some breakfast at 11 the following morning. She hadn't eaten so late in months.

The next night he called at around 8. He asked her if she wanted him to come over, but she suggested she walk over to his place instead. When she arrived at his building, a woman in the lobby let her inside, looking her up and down. The woman was black. Sara didn't realize there were buildings in the village or nearby that rented largely to African Americans. He shrugged when she asked him about it. Then he smiled, like a Cheshire cat.

"I bet you don't think about a building being largely 'white' when you get your mail and run into a neighbor," he said, eyebrows raised.

"No, I don't. Or haven't. Guess I'm going to learn all sorts of things because of what we're doing," she responded, a frown on her face. But Michael was not going to allow her to go there.

"Speaking of what we're doing," he began, taking her hand after slipping off her jacket. "Let me show you the decorations in my boudoir."

"Such a big word," she said, looking very serious. When she saw the purple bedspread she smiled broadly. "Did you get this before or after?"

"You don't think I have a mind of my own?" he asked. "Besides, it's not lavender." Then he pushed her down on it, saying, "Stop talking." He covered her face, her mouth, her breasts with kisses. Wet and sloppy which made her laugh. She stopped laughing when the kisses became real and deep and exciting.

"Oh my," she sighed. He was going to ask what happened to 'oh

Tingle

God' but was already committed and didn't want to ruin the mood. He removed her sweater very gently when she wanted to tear off his.

Soon they were naked. When she reached for his very erect penis, he said, "Not yet. I just want to look at you."

She lay there, suddenly shy.

"Your breasts are beautiful. A perfect size, with nipples that stand up all by themselves."

"Not usually…" she said, and then kept quiet because he had put a finger across her lips.

"Open your legs," he demanded.

She complied, though she felt quite vulnerable. "Wider," he again demanded."

Then he leaned over and began stroking, plunging a finger deep inside her. "You're very wet," he told her. All Sara could do was groan.

With very quick, light, circular strokes of his fingers, he began to bring her to climax.

When she protested, mildly, "But I want you inside," he again put his finger to her mouth. "We have plenty of time." She slipped the finger into her mouth, which made him gasp. "I've never tasted myself before…," she said. Then his head was between her wide-open legs and he was licking and then gently sucking.

"Oh God."

"That-a girl," he whispered, and then she came, crying out loud.

"I hope your neighbor wasn't asleep," she muttered, even more embarrassed. Then he was stroking her again, murmuring 'Twice is better than once."

He was staring at her pudenda, fascinated, as he used first his fingers and then his mouth. "So pink," he managed, and then it sounded like he was gulping.

"I'm coming again...."she moaned.

"I know," he agreed. "Have you ever come twice like this before?"

All Sara could do was shake her head. Jeffrey hadn't eaten her out all that often. She hadn't missed it, and had never even realized how much she relished the touch of a tongue.

Sara reached for him, moaning 'please, please.'

"Anything you want," he smiled, entering her easily, and then they were moving in unison, very slowly, wanting to extend the experience, the minutes, the hour, the time – until they could no longer contain themselves.

"I'm...going...to...come!" she sighed.

"So...am...I!" he all but screamed, and then they did, together.

When he started to roll over, she held him back. "Oh no. Your body feels wonderful, and you're still inside me."

"But I'm soft," he murmured.

"Not completely," she disagreed. "See, you're getting hard again.

Neither said another word, as they rocked together, and then began to move their hips quickly, with more urgency. When they both came again, Sara first and then Michael seconds later, he didn't think he could have rolled off of her even if she had asked.

Finally he murmured, "I'm going to crush you," and rolled. This time she didn't object, instead teasing, "You already have.

The following morning Michael left before Sara, who was completely startled when he handed her a set of keys for his apartment as she sat on the side of his bed.

"I've never given these to another woman," he admitted shyly. "I had them made yesterday."

Tingle

Sara stood on her tiptoes and kissed him gently on his lips. "I'm honored," she whispered. They held each other for a few seconds, and then he left.

A few days later after Sara had again spent the night, once she had showered, dressed and cleaned up the few dishes they had used for breakfast, she found his keys in her purse and smiled. Then she opened the door, debating whether to stop at Citarella on her way home to stock up on kale, broccoli, apples and other healthy favorites. She was so absorbed in her thoughts, she didn't notice Michael's neighbor, who had seemed displeased to see her with him just a few days before.

"Hi," she said without thinking. "I'm Sara."

The other woman's eyes opened wide, and she replied, because she clearly didn't know what else to do, "And I'm Cheryl."

Neither could decide what else to say. "Michael thought you might want to have a glass of wine with us over the weekend," Sara blurted, although he had suggested no such thing. The other woman was completely nonplussed. She had noticed Michael when she had moved into the building over a year before, and despite several efforts at 'friendship', had been rebuffed.

"Um...sure," she muttered. "How about Friday night? I may be going out of town for the weekend on Saturday with some girlfriends."

Sara replied with a smile. "I'll ask Michael if that works and slip a note under your door."

She had done the right thing. The last thing she needed was an enemy right next door to her...whatever Michael was.

Cheryl turned to go as quickly as she could, as startled as Sara by the offer. 'Maybe the man just likes white women,' she thought as she hurried to the subway station.

Nancy Alvarez

As Sara perused the organic vegetables at her favorite small village market, she started to feel chest pains, making it difficult for her to breathe evenly. She hadn't had a panic attack in years, but knew one when she felt it. She took some calming breaths – it took many – paid for the groceries, and plucked her cell phone from her purse as soon as she walked outside the store.

She needed to talk to someone, and speed dialed Lucy. Lucy was a freelance writer and worked at home, so she was the logical choice. She had also been Sara's friend since their college days at Barnard. Sara only had to utter a few words for her old friend to realize something significant had occurred.

Chapter 3

"Where do you want to meet?" Lucy asked. "Or should I just come to your apartment?"

"Come on over. I'll put up a pot of coffee," Sara replied with relief. She knew talking in a public place about what was happening in her love life would be beyond her.

"I'll stop at Murray's. Do you have cream cheese?"

Since Sara had no idea – she couldn't even remember when she had last eaten bagels and cream cheese in her condo – she told Lucy to bring some bagels too. She did know she had raspberry preserves in her frig.

By the time she arrived, Sara had put up a pot of coffee, taken out plates, silverware and napkins, poured lo-fat milk that was about to expire into a pitcher, and sat down on the couch. Every few minutes she jumped up to look through the peephole in her front door to see if her friend was walking down the hall. She was pacing the living room when the bell finally rang, which completely startled her. How had Lucy gotten into the lobby without pressing the buzzer to be allowed upstairs? Probably a neighbor had let her in.

"How weird," her friend said as she carried her bag of bagels and cream cheese into the kitchen. 'You look radiant but totally exhausted. By the way, I got some nova scotia too, since I hadn't had any in a long time."

"Neither have I," Sara agreed. "And I am exhausted. That's why I asked you to come over."

"Shall we wait until we're sitting down to eat, or do you want to start while I unload everything onto plates and carry them into the dining room?" Lucy asked calmly, though she was obviously quite curious.

Sara sighed. "I can pat my head and rub my tummy at the same time. At least I used to be able to," she muttered. When she didn't begin talking, but instead reached for the bagel bag so she could dump them into the basket she had put on the counter, Lucy turned to her and demanded, "Well…?"

"Oh God," sigh. "Well, here goes." Again Sara paused.

"This must be momentous," Lucy teased.

"Remember the good looking black librarian we were talking about the other day," Sara asked.

"Who could forget him?" Lucy groaned. "And you even got to have wine with him!" She looked at her old college friend expectantly.

Never one to mince words, Sara said, "I'm sleeping with him!"

"What?" Lucy shrieked. "Oh my God. Is he as good in bed as we thought he would be? Is it true what they say about black men?

Tingle

The only black man I ever fooled around with was in high school – a bad boy – but we never managed to get his cock out of his pants."

Sara couldn't help but laugh. "Yes, the rumor's true, at least with him."

"Oh God, why didn't I ever flirt with him?" Lucy asked, though not seriously.

"Yeah right," Sara grinned. "Like that was ever a possibility." Both women knew she adored her husband, Jordan.

"You didn't think he was a possibility either, despite what it felt like when he put his hand on your back. We've both just liked salivating over him. It was all a fantasy, or that's what I thought," Lucy replied as she carried the bagels, cream cheese and lox to the table. Then she returned to the kitchen to pour the coffee, directing Sara to sit before she 'fell down'. "Wow," she added as she, too, sat down.

"One day about six weeks ago, we were talking about books the way we always have, when he…or was it me…I don't remember. Yes I do; it was me, at least the second time. I couldn't believe it when the words came out of my mouth, but I suggested we go have wine, even though it wasn't our usual day," Sara sighed.

"He could tell I wasn't feeling great – some days are still worse than others, and he immediately said 'of course' He said he'd call his trainer and cancel."

"Hmm. I knew there was a reason I've always liked the guy. What a nice thing to do. Where'd you go?" she asked, always one for details.

"To the same wine bar on 8th Street," Sara said. "But nothing happened then. Well, not really true. He asked great questions, and I answered and then asked him stuff, and then we realized we'd been sitting there again for a couple of hours."

"Amazing!" Lucy declared with delight at her old friend's good fortune.

"It was. It is," Sara agreed. 'It was,' she thought to herself. It really was. But could she talk about the rest, even with Luce...?'

Lucy reached across the table, butter knife loaded with cream cheese in her left hand, and laid her other hand over Sara's. "You can tell me whatever you want. There's no judgment between us. Never has been."

"I've never behaved this way," Sara admitted.

"That sounds interesting. What the hell do you mean?" Lucy asked.

And Sara began to describe sex with Michael. "I want to lick every part of him," she began. "And he doesn't mind. Actually, he seems to feel the same way."

"Doesn't that tickle?" Lucy blurted.

"Oh no. Sometimes the feel of his tongue on my wrist makes me come," Sara replied, eyes wide. "Well almost."

"You always said sex with Jeffrey was great," Lucy said.

"It was. I did…. But it wasn't like this. Sex has never been like this. And Jeffrey, with Jeffrey there was so much love."

"And not here?"

"I don't think we know each other well enough to feel love," Sara replied with some embarrassment.

"But you know each other well enough to be licking each other?"

Lucy always had had a great sense of humor. Making a joke about it somehow lessened Sara's discomfort.

"One night we had both just come, but he stayed on top of me, and then I realized he was getting hard again," Sara said.

Lucy's mouth actually dropped open. "Now that I've never experienced."

"Neither of us had either. Or so he said later."

Tingle

"Did you both come again? How could he have? I thought that was impossible," Lucy rattled on, totally in awe.

"Me too. Isn't that amazing!" Sara declared, not a question because she knew it was.

"So is he the best sexual partner you've ever had?" Lucy asked.

Ashamed that it wasn't Jeffrey, she merely shook her head 'yes'.

"I slept with one black guy..." Lucy began, interrupted by 'you did?' because she had never told Sara.

"He wasn't a particularly sensitive lover, but he sure was big!" Lucy laughed.

"Fortunately Michael is both!" Sara declared, setting both women into peels of laughter.

"If I'd paid more attention to my neighbor a couple of years ago, maybe I would have asked him to go for coffee," Lucy mused.

"As if you'd ever cheat on Jordan," Sara said, her tone making it clear that would never happen.

"Silly me," Lucy quipped.

"Like hell! You and Jordan are almost as good together as Jeffrey and I were," Sara said and then laughed again.

"Ha ha ha ha!" Lucy responded. "At least Jordan likes oral sex! I always heard black guys didn't, and the one I tried sure didn't."

"That's a myth too," Sara declared, to which her friend groaned, "It's just not fair."

The women cleaned up together, and then Lucy rushed off to her early afternoon exercise class, which she said was going to be painful because she was so full.

At dinner a few nights later Michael suggested they move in together. Sara was unnerved. She hesitated, and he mistook her reticence.

"I know my place is smaller. We could use yours, but I didn't want to presume," he explained.

"I'm not sure I'm ready to live with you, Michael," Sara admitted with some hesitation. "At either of our apartments."

Michael shrugged, trying not to look disappointed, though it was quite obvious that he was. He made excuses about why he couldn't spend the night, and left.

Sara picked up her phone and called Lucy, who asked her, "Why do you think you're not ready?"

Sighing, Sara replied, "Maybe it's just about sex."

Lucy assured her that was not how it had sounded to her. After all, the whole thing had begun with discussions about novels. Not a terribly sexy subject.

"But we rarely discuss much of anything any more. We're too busy taking off our clothes," Sara mumbled.

"Lucky you," Lucy said. It was her turn to sigh. Passion had to change over time. She couldn't expect to be tearing at Jordan's clothes after all these years. She took a sip of wine and continued, "You know, I think I have an idea."

"What's that?" asked Sara.

"Why don't you return to the beginning, talking about books and other topics that interest you both, instead of just hopping into the sack. You could even forego an occasional roll in the hay."

Laughing, Sara replied, "Aside from the last part, that actually seems like a very good idea. Then I think I could even explain why I'm hesitating."

"See? It's not just about sex. If it was, he'd never understand, and you know he would, " Lucy suggested.

Tingle

Sara thought about Lucy's remark after they had hung up, even while she was brushing her teeth.

The next evening, after she and Michael had spent more than an hour in her bed, she whispered, "I love this so much…."

No intuitive slouch, Michael immediately responded, "But…"

"I miss the friendship part of us. I mean, that's how all this started," she reminded him.

"Actually I do too," he agreed, surprising her.

"What do we do about it?" she asked him.

"We make an effort to do more than this," he said immediately, adding with a grin, "Even though that won't be so easy." She smiled but didn't say anything because she could tell he was thinking about it. "There's an arts lecture at the 92nd Street Y on Friday. Why don't I get tickets," he suggested.

Sara's smile was almost as large as Michael's usual grin. "What a great idea! Who's lecturing and what's he talking about?" she asked.

Michael's smile answered hers. "It's a woman, you chauvinist, and she's going to be talking about Chagall."

"I like Chagall. Even better," she sighed with relief at being understood.

"Does that mean we have to let up on this part?" he asked in mock seriousness. At which point, she rolled over on top of him, asking, "What do you think?"

Their second take was slower, almost languorous. With her knees on either side of his body, her tongue began its slow descent down his chest to his belly. By the time she reached his cock he was moaning, which was at least part of her intention.

"You get hard so easily," she murmured.

"Not all the time," he said with a gasp.

"With me!" she looked up, utterly delighted.

"It's gonna take longer this time," he managed to say before he gave in to the shivers she was inspiring with the action of her tongue and lips.

"Good. Then you'll be able to service me too!"

At that, despite her actions, he burst out laughing. "Service?" he gasped.

"You bet," she replied, the tip of his penis in her mouth.

"At your service," he quipped before he couldn't even mumble anything else.

By the time he had come inside her after playing with her clitoris with his fingers and then his tongue, both of them were utterly spent. Sara came while he was tonguing her, and then came again seconds after he did, collapsing next to her on the guestroom bed. In the morning he wanted to bring up the possibility of their living together, but decided to wait, at least for a month. He was crazy about this woman, even if she was white, he thought to himself several times during his workday.

The small Chagall exhibit in the lecture hall was awesome, the woman's talk almost as good as the paintings themselves. Neither of them had actually seen any of his work at a museum, and both were dumbstruck by the colors and shapes. The following week they went to a play off-Broadway, this time choosing the venue and purchasing the tickets together. The theater was closer to his apartment than to her condo, so they walked there quickly, not because it was late, but because they were each thinking about the other's body. Doing things together had done nothing to sate their passion.

They made it into his tiny foyer, but Michael pulled her down right there on the little rectangular African rug, his first purchase as an adult. It had followed him from his first studio apartment to the next and finally, to this one. She pulled at his belt buckle when he was shedding his fall jacket, and then his pants were around his ankles and off. Her panties came next, and then he was inside, moving up and down and then side-to-side, which they had discovered weeks before drove her wild.

"We should slow down," he panted, but she shook her head 'no', gasping, "We have tomorrow."

A few weeks later she ran into one of her neighbors as she was saying goodbye to Michael outside her building. He jogged off with a wave, and the woman raised her eyebrows at Sara, and just stood there.

"Jeffrey's been gone for more than a year," Sara reminded her.

"That isn't why I'm staring at you," said the neighbor without any shame.

"Oh for God's sake. In New York City?" Sara glared.

"What does that have to do with anything?" the woman retorted.

"We're kind of a multi-racial city, don't you think?" Sara asked with obvious disdain.

The neighbor, whose name Sara could not recall, shrugged.

"So we can live on the same block, but that's it?" Sara demanded, adding, "Shame on you."

"I sure wouldn't date one," the woman muttered as she turned to walk away.

"Do you have any black friends?" Sara asked the woman's retreating back, her fury knowing no bounds.

"Not that kind of friend," the woman said over her shoulder. Conversation closed. Sara decided not to tell Michael about the incident. He didn't need that kind of grief, especially if he moved into her building.

Nancy Alvarez

No other neighbor in the small brownstone said a word to her, or as far as she knew, to him. She still seethed inside, and was having a hard time letting go of her anger a week later. As they made dinner side by side the following week, Michael said, "OK. I thought you'd tell me what was wrong, but you haven't. So now I'm asking."

She sighed. "I didn't want to talk to you about it." And then she told him the whole sorry tale.

He shrugged. "A few of your neighbors have talked to me at your mailbox when I've gone down in the morning to get your mail. No problem."

"I thought it'd bother you more. That's why I didn't say anything," she admitted.

Another shrug. "I've lived with this a pretty long time, Sara. Being black. I'm always careful, but I accept friendliness when it's offered."

"I guess there's no point not to," she agreed.

"If I got mad every time someone behaved like that woman did – which apartment is she in, by the way? – I'd be a basket case," he explained.

"She's on the third floor. Front unit. We've barely even spoken to each other before, and yet she still felt she could say what she did. That's what's so amazing," she fumed.

"Nothing racial is amazing, my sweet. It's part of this country," he grimaced.

"I know. But I've never had to deal with it directly before. I'm ashamed my liberal Jewish tuches didn't 'know' if you know what I mean," she said.

"Knowing and 'knowing' are two totally different animals," he agreed. "I presume tuches means derriere."

"I want to know everything," she fumed. "And yes, it does."

Tingle

"Red flames are coming out of the top of your head," he laughed. "You want to know everything about what?"

"Everything about that part of your life. What your parents taught you about how to cope. How you did. And is that why you've only dated black women?" she added as an afterthought.

"This may take years," he suggested, a twinkle in his eye.

"Probably," she agreed, desperately holding back tears. What in the world was wrong with her?

He brushed her face with his long, gentle fingers. Then he kissed each of her eyes, and next, her lips.

But she stopped him. "Uh-uh. You can't get away from this discussion that easily."

"I'm not trying to. But it probably will take years to really explain, and for you to understand," he murmured.

"You could start by telling me just one thing," she suggested, looking directly into his soft brown eyes.

"My father told me I always had to be careful around white folks when I was four," he said. "I wasn't sure what he meant, but I sure knew why by then."

"Careful how?" she asked him.

"Exactly."

Sara looked at him quizzically.

Michael looked back at her, his features shrouded in sadness. "If I said that to anyone black, they would know instantly."

"I realize that. But I'm white, if you hadn't noticed, and I really do want to know," she replied. She then reached down for his hand.

He sighed. "If I walked into an A & P with you, more people than not would stare at me, even after we passed them."

"Are you sure you're not being paranoid?" she asked as gently as she knew how.

"Nope. Ask my black neighbor, the one who gave you the dirty look," he replied with a very sad grin.

"I see quite a few interracial couples in the City, especially in the Village...."

"Do you watch them when they pass by," he asked quite seriously.

"I don't think so. I don't know," she replied, feeling very sad. "Are you sorry we started talking about this?"

"Nope," he answered with no hesitation at all. "Are you?"

"God no," she sighed.

Again he thought of bringing up the subject of them living together, but refrained. Over wine a few days later, he decided it was time. "I really do think we should live together," he began. Her eyes became even larger, but she didn't immediately respond. He waited patiently, his face impassive, another trait he had learned at his father's knee. This he didn't tell Sara.

"Wow!" she finally exhaled. "I think we should too, but it feels very scary."

"Because I'm black?" he asked quite seriously.

"Oh please," she exclaimed. "Give me a break."

"Well," he smiled. "That was direct."

At that, Sara laughed. "I've been told I'm too direct my whole life."

"By Jeffrey?" Michael asked her.

"Not very often. Sometimes," she admitted with obvious reticence.

Michael rose, going into his kitchen and coming back with another bottle of wine, which he was uncorking. "I think this discussion calls for another, don't you?"

Tingle

Smiling, she gave a shake of her head. "So," she then said. "My place or yours?"

"AS I said, I think mine is too small, if we're going to try this," he said. Sensing the reason for her hesitation, he added, "We can turn the guest room into our bedroom."

"No," she demurred. "I think it's time for me to let go. How about painting the whole condo?"

Michael groaned, which she didn't expect. "Now we're going to have to agree on colors…."

"That's true. We could do off white, or whatever they call that color, and then accent walls in the bedroom and living room," she mused.

"How about light blue, with a navy accent wall," he thought aloud.

"Just in the bedroom, I presume," she asked.

"Yup. Not sure about the living room yet."

And thus the decision was made. They fell asleep enfolded in each other's arms. In the morning both realized they had chosen to take a very big step with one another. Was it the right move? Neither brought it up again.

As soon as she walked in her front door, soon to be their front door, Sara picked up her landline because she hated holding her cell phone to her ear, sure she was subjecting herself to ear cancer, if there was such a thing. This was not going to be a short conversation.

"I'm thrilled," gushed Lucy. "I know this is the right move. He's not only a hunk, he's lovely as well! Wow, you did it," she marveled.

"I think I'm thrilled too, but I keep walking through these rooms seeing Jeffrey in my mind. In the bedroom of course, and in the living room reading his daily New York Times…"

Lucy interrupted her. "Stop it. Right now. Jeffrey would want you to have someone you care about in your life."

"In our condo?" Sara asked her.

"Why not? He's long gone, and don't berate me for saying that. It's true," Lucy declared. "Wow, how exciting!"

Sara gulped in air but didn't say anything.

Lucy continued with a question. "Do you think anyone else in the building will care that you're living with a black man?"

Sara replied, "He's already talked to several people at the mailboxes when he'd gone down to get my mail, and they seemed friendly, or so he said," she explained.

Lucy laughed. "He has no reason to lie, sweetie. You know, it is New York City, and the West Village. Who would give a shit?"

"The woman who gave me a hard time," Sara muttered.

"Do you really care what that asshole thinks?" her friend asked her. "Show some spunk, girl. You're going to be living with someone you've had the best sex of your life with, and who you really like on top of that!"

"We're going to repaint the apartment," Sara said, a non sequitur if ever there was one.

"You have to be excited. I am. Have you decided on colors?" she asked Sara.

"Light blue with a navy accent wall in the bedroom. Haven't come up with anything for the living room yet," Sara sighed. So much to figure out.

"Don't you dare sigh. This has to be exciting, damn it. How about light yellow for the kitchen?" Lucy asked.

"I think he'd like that," Sara agreed.

"Him!" her friend screamed. "How about you?"

Tingle

"Remember my first apartment on 10th Street. You and I painted the kitchen light yellow," Sara reminded her.

"Oh yeah. That we did. You could use plain old linen white in the living room so you can hang up his pictures and yours," Lucy continued.

"Oh God, something else to figure out. And what do I do about the posters Jeffrey and I chose years ago?" Sara was not enjoying this.

"Toss the ones you never really liked, and talk to Michael about the others. See how he feels about living with stuff you bought with your husband," Lucy replied without any hesitation.

"How do I make this fun?" Sara groaned.

"Picture him eating your pussy," Lucy laughed. At that, Sara started to laugh too. "That's an idea," she managed to gulp out.

As it happened, Lucy had a friend moving into the City who was looking for a short sublet until she found a permanent apartment in an area she wanted to live in. This made Sara much more comfortable about Michael moving into her loft. If cohabiting proved less than perfect, he would be able to move back into his own place. If they liked, or even loved, living together, he would have time to find a long-term tenant, and tell his landlord what he was doing. If the man could meet the 'new' renter and vet her or him, he would probably let Michael sublet. Michael had never been late with a rental payment in the four years he had lived in the building, the landlord often calling him 'his best tenant'.

The day Michael began moving boxes into Sara's condo, they barely got two of them in the front door before they fell to the carpet in her foyer and began kissing, touching, and taking off clothes. Their first sexual encounter in their joint space was in the hallway, not even in the newly painted master bedroom. That night, after they changed the sheets to a set of Michael's together, laughing as they did so, they again made love, this time in a more languorous fashion because of their earlier indulgence.

He brushed his tongue down the length of her, from neck to toe, stopping for a nibble at her parted nether lips, but not completing the job, not until he had taken each of her toes into his mouth. Then he mad his way back up to her pussy, doing what he did best until she came with a loud outcry. Had the walls in the brownstone not been so thick, Sara told him she never would have left the place again.

"You mean I would have to do all the shopping?" he asked with a chuckle.

"Don't forget the cleaning," she reminded him, and he quipped, "You'll be able to do that since you won't be leaving here ever again."

They laughed together, wrapped in one another's arms, both falling asleep with a smile. When Michael woke her up with his exploring tongue in the morning, she almost mumbled that she was too tired, but then he dissuaded her with his fingers and his cock, which slipped inside her quite easily.

"I'm sopping, aren't I?" she asked him.

"Oh yeah," came his happy reply as their hips took up their familiar rhythm. She came before he did despite thinking she was too tired. With Michael, that didn't ever seem to be the case. As she drifted back into sleep she heard him whistling at the front door and sighed with contentment.

Later she walked through the freshly painted rooms she had shared with Jeffrey for over twenty years, realizing it no longer looked like their home. It wasn't exactly hers and Michael's yet either, but in time, she told herself, after he had fully moved in, that change would happen as well. Michael wanted to pack more boxes, so the following

Tingle

night they each stayed at their respective places. As she was falling asleep Sara wondered if they both unconsciously wanted at least one more night in their 'own' space before they took this very large and new step. She still slept like a baby. She had accepted that Michael was the man in her life. Time would tell if that would be permanent.

Chapter 4

By the weekend, all of his boxes were either sitting in the foyer or stacked near Sara's bookcases in the living room, none left behind at his old apartment. Lucy's friend had moved her boxes in to his apartment by Saturday night. Their decision to live in her condo was final, at least for the few months the woman would be inhabiting his apartment. They both assumed his landlord would not realize he was not living there because he lived in New Jersey and rarely visited the building. Michael had told his super that he would be out of town for a couple of months and a woman friend would be staying in his place until she found an apartment of her own. The man didn't seem distressed by the news, and told him to have a good time. Michael pictured Sara and assured the man he would.

He grinned all the way to her condo.

Their lovemaking that Saturday was particularly passionate because each of them wanted to bless the move they were making. When Sara finally took his cock into her mouth, his hands gripped her shoulders. He couldn't stop moaning.

"I didn't think you could get any harder…or bigger," she chuckled and then took him in her mouth again.

"Oh Jesus! Oh God," he called out. And then, "I can't hold out." She then used her hand as well as her mouth and he exploded.

"Yum," she whispered.

"I'm too spent to even laugh," he muttered. "Oh God. You really are something!"

"So are you. If you wake up in the middle of the night, don't hesitate," she said. "I can't believe I've become so brazen."

"Keep it up," he murmured, as he drifted off to dreamland. Then, "Oh, I guess it's me who does that."

She did laugh then, but he didn't hear her. He was already sound asleep. The next thing she felt was Michael spooning her, and slipping easily inside. She opened her eyes; it was dark out; she could tell by the crack below the bedroom shade. It was still dark when they finished. The very idea of what he was doing, entering her while she slept, was so exciting she, too, came without any manual stimulation.

"Aren't you naughty," she mumbled as she started to drift off.

"It was your suggestion," he reminded her and then both were again asleep.

On Sunday she made them a big breakfast with eggs, bacon, sautéed vegies and two large toasted everything-bagels from Katz's. He told her he could unpack himself, but Sara wouldn't hear of it.

"I'd feel ridiculous reading my Sunday Times while you slaved away over your boxes. Oops, sorry. Just an expression," she grimaced.

"Yeah right," he turned his head, looking mock angry. "Now I know what you really have in mind."

"Yup. But I had in mind a sex slave, not the other kind," she quipped as she carried his shaving kit into the master bathroom.

"I'm all yours!" he yelled from the other room.

When they were making room for his books on her bookshelves, reorganizing so the books on the shelves would still be in alphabetical order – a quirk of Sara's that Michael easily understood, given his profession – she shyly said, "I didn't really think this would work."

Affectionately Michael patted the top of her head. "And why was that?"

"Because you're a darky!" she retorted, making him laugh. "Seriously though, because the sex seems so important."

"Isn't it?" he asked her.

"Yes, it is. But…" she wasn't sure how to finish and not sound insulting.

"Intimacy is growing too, don't you think?" he held her chin in his hand so he could look into her eyes.

"Yes," she had to agree, adding, almost as an afterthought, "I grew up in Eastchester, where most people were pretty straight."

"No darkies there," he quickly retorted, surprised when she burst out laughing.

"Nope. Certainly not when I was growing up there," she again agreed when she could stop laughing. Both continued to unpack his books and slip them into their correct places on her bookshelves.

"Wow," Sara murmured. "Our upbringing's actually something we need to talk about, don't you think?"

He took the books she was holding and then her hand, leading her over to her soft and wonderfully comfortable couch. "Yes, we do."

Gently Michael reminded her, "At least you dated a black guy once upon a time. I've never even had white women friends."

"Have you had any white male friends," she asked, genuinely curious.

"Over the years, one or two. But it isn't as easy with them," he added. "And that could have been my fault."

"Lack of trust," she said, understanding immediately.

Michael sighed. "Probably. Plus there were things that were just too hard to explain."

Totally serious, Sara asked, "Are you willing to try explaining all of that, over time, to me?"

He sighed again. "Yes. Although I may be crazy."

"Doing this? Maybe we both are, but here we are."

Then he smiled his wonderful, full grin that took over his entire face. "Time flies when you're having fun."

"Speaking of fun…" she began.

"And this is why I think I may have made a mistake, at least about white women," he laughed, reaching for the buttons on her blouse.

"We've never done this here before," she whispered. Once she was naked, and Michael wearing just his jockeys, he got up from the couch and headed for the bathroom. "I think we better use a towel," he turned back to explain.

"Ah," she sighed.

When he returned, her fingers were playing with her clitoris.

Michael gasped, "Don't stop. Let me see."

She was pretty excited by then, and amazed. "Never done this in front of anyone before either."

"Embarrassed?" he asked her.

Tingle

"Not really. Amazing," she gasped again, close to coming. When she was done, she thought Michael would lie down beside her, but instead he knelt by the couch, his tongue drawing circles around her clitoris.

"Oh my God, Michael!"

"You are so wet," he said, tongue still swirling.

This time when she came, she yelled out loud. Michael sat on his haunches, grinning with pride. "Can I lie down yet?" he teased. Sara held out her arms, and they lay entwined on the couch, the towel he had brought to put beneath them on the floor.

"I have so many questions," she murmured, limp from the two orgasms.

"Go ahead. Ask away," he replied, voice slow and languorous, eyes lidded but alert.

"Where did you grow up?" was her first question.

"Newark," he replied. "In the hood."

"What did your parents do?" her second. She was startled to realize Michael suddenly looked embarrassed.

"My mother could have cleaned your house, but Eastchester was a little far from Newark," he finally replied.

After awhile she murmured. "And here we are."

"Thank God," he sighed.

"Yes. Thank God," she agreed.

Then he asked, "Do you feel guilty?"

She shook her head 'no', surprised. "When I was a little girl, the kid up the block and I were curious what we looked like. So I suggested one of us put a leg up on the toilet seat, and the other one kneel and look up. I went first."

"Did anyone ever find out?" he asked, both startled and a bit amused.

"That's the important part of the story. Her mom walked in on us," Sara mumbled, looking away. Michael knew no more jokes were in order.

"What happened?" he asked with a tenderness that almost brought her to tears.

"The woman called me a filthy child and kicked me out of the house. After that whenever her daughter saw me she crossed the street." Michael wiped away the tears that had begun to dribble down her cheeks. "My mom told me I wasn't a dirty little girl. That wanting to look, and even touch, was perfectly normal, though she sure didn't seem happy."

"That's still an amazing response in the fifties," he said with some surprise.

"Yes," she shook her head. "I really loved my mom, except when she was a pain in the ass."

He grinned. "And when was that?"

"When she judged me. She could be pretty judgmental," Sara replied.

"Not when it counted," he suggested.

"No. I think I inherited my best traits from her," she concurred.

Back to teasing, he tickled her. "Even in the sack?"

Sara had to laugh. "I don't think she ever experienced anything like this," she said. "Though once she told me that my father would often fall asleep 'down there'. I was driving and almost crashed into a tree."

"Holy shit! What an interesting woman," he said.

"That she was. Your turn now," she replied, obviously wanting to change the subject.

"I'll ask about your father another day," he agreed.

"Yes please!"

Tingle

They lay side by side, both content in the silence. Then Michael said, "OK. Here goes. My Dad was very strict. He was a postman. Passing the test was a really big deal, and he only took it because my mother pushed him, convinced he was smart enough to pass."

"Women rule!" declared Sara with a smile.

"Ha ha," he groused.

"Could you talk to him about what was important in your life?" she then asked.

"Not really," he replied, sadness in his voice.

"What about your mom?" Sara asked quietly, almost afraid to pose the question.

"Yeah, I could talk to my mom," he replied, and then turned his head to smile at her.

"Even about sex?" she asked, incredulous.

"Of course not," he replied. "That I learned about from the older boys at school."

"Junior high?" came her immediate question.

Somewhat embarrassed, he answered, "Elementary."

"Wow, very advanced," she shrugged.

"That's the hood for you," he said, shrugging in turn.

Sara had all sorts of other questions as well: did they eat dinner together as a family? (yes); did he hang out with a particular group of boys? (yes to that too); did his parents approve of his friends? (yes, his mom; no, his dad); and when she questioned him further: who didn't your father approve of and why, he told her that was a longer discussion.

"We have all night," she responded, burying under the covers.

"You are relentless, lady," he sighed.

"Yup. So Jeffrey always told me. Get used to it," she laughed.

"At least it comes with perks," he joked.

57

"Big perks," she agreed.

Michael continued, albeit with reluctance. "I kind of gravitated to the tough kids since I was bookish. They had more to teach me."

"Did you try to explain that to your dad?" she asked.

"To my mom. My Dad would have probably called me a sissy," he said with a sigh. She understood talking about his dad was really difficult for him.

"Maybe that's why you like women," Sara suggested, changing tacks.

"Probably. Though I learned about women by experimentation," he explained.

"Lucky for me," she grinned. Michael pulled her close.

"Will your mom approve of us?" she then asked, fearing the answer. "Shouldn't we drive out to Jersey, since we've moved in together?"

Michael's response was immediate. "She'll like you. A lot. But she may also caution me about dating a white woman, let alone getting serious with one."

"Moving into my condo won't seem a good idea to her," Sara mused.

He agreed. "But she'll be relieved that I didn't give up my place."

"Maybe you should go see her first, to get her used to the idea," Sara murmured.

"I'll think about it."

Again they fell silent. Michael rolled over so he was facing her. Again, she felt that familiar tingle.

"Back to you," he murmured. "What do you do with your time every day?"

Sara frowned. "It's going to sound very privileged."

Tingle

"Go for it," he urged, although he was again wondering what he was doing with this woman whose background was so different from his own.

"I meet my friends for lunch – yuck, that really sounds like some PBS series," she groaned. "I exercise," she continued, but he interrupted.

"I know. Your body's very tight," he agreed, running his hands down the length of her, giving particular attention to her breasts.

"I don't think you want me to answer. Not if you're doing what you're doing." She barely managed to get the words out.

"I don't want to stop, but I do want to hear what you do, so I'll just stop for awhile," he grinned.

Taking a deep breath, Sara said, "I've started an outline for a novel."

Michael was both fascinated and startled. "Wow, a novel. I'm impressed."

"Don't be. I doubt it's very good," came her immediate response.

Sternly, he reprimanded her. "Don't do that."

"I'll try not to. OK. It's about two different families, one from the Ukraine, and one from cultured Vienna, based loosely on my family," she said, adding, "I did a lot of research."

"How?" he asked the obvious question.

"A librarian at 42nd Street suggested a book called 'There Once Was A World' to me. It's about life in a shtetl – that's a tiny rural Jewish village. Then I talked to my cousin about what her mom had told her about her mother's life in Vienna."

"That's really interesting, though I'm insulted you didn't ask your favorite librarian for help," he frowned.

"The librarian uptown is Jewish," she explained.

"I get it, but I'm still sorry," he told her, meaning it.

"If I need more information, I'll just ask my lover," she smiled.

"Isn't he more than that?" Michael asked.

"Much more."

He held her face lightly between his hands before he said, "So are you."

"It's a lot to take in. Doesn't it scare you, just a little?" Sara didn't want to be the only one who was sometimes unable to sleep, worrying about what she was doing.

Surprised to realize it didn't, he told her so. Then he asked what her childhood was like. She talked about being bored in school, but reading 'other' books the local librarian suggested. "You see, librarians have always had an important role in my life."

He wanted to know what books the librarian in Eastchester had recommended to her.

"Laura Ingles Wilder, Willa Cather, the 'Betsy, Tacy and Tib' novels by Maud Hart Lovelace. And when she told me it was time for me to graduate to the adult section, the first book I read was 'Gentlemen's Agreement.'"

He smiled. "No wonder you like librarians."

"Will you still suggest books to me?" she teased, although he answered in all seriousness, "Of course."

She sighed with contentment and then continued. "I loved to roller skate. You know, the kind of skates you attached to your shoes with a skate key," she added.

He shrugged, "Being a city boy, I never saw those. And I guess none of the girls in my neighborhood could have afforded them anyway."

"My parents were always worried about money," she said, feeling a need to explain, "And skates weren't very expensive. They kept me busy for hours. My sister got a baseball bat, used, and a ball."

Tingle

"Was your father OK with you and your sister being athletic?" he wondered.

Sara shrugged. "Don't know. He never said anything about it. He left early in the morning for his drug store every day, and when he came home we were already inside watching 'The Magic Cottage."

"The Magic Cottage?"

"A kids show. Suburban kids show…"

"White kids," he interrupted.

"Yup. With a white woman and puppets. But unlike Sesame Street as I recall the puppets were either white, or animals," she admitted. "I never gave it much thought. I guess none of us kids did back then. I didn't until I got to college. Then I gave it a lot of thought and joined marches, protests…."

"Which your father must have loved," he frowned.

"Oh yeah. He had no idea what to do with me," Sara concurred.

"Maybe it's a good idea he's not still around. This, you and me, it might kill him if he wasn't already dead," he mused.

"And my mother would have liked you. As I said," she sighed. "And I can understand why both of our mothers would have been worried about us."

"So can I. And I can see why I never tried it before," he mumbled.

Her eyes filled, and he kissed the tears away. They lay in her bed, face to face.

"I was called rebel-with-a-cause in high school. He sure hated that," Sara mused. "I didn't protest yet; that came later, when I was on my own in college."

"Did your father know what you were doing then?" he asked, curious.

"Don't know," she shrugged. "I didn't talk to either one of my parents about it. And then I met Jeffrey, who came from an affluent Jewish family, so there was nothing to talk about."

He chuckled, "So much for the rebel," which annoyed her no end.

"We fell in love, for God's sake. And we had a sustaining marriage for almost twenty years that had nothing to do with our mutual, and un-practiced, religion," she scowled. "Don't do that," she warned.

"What?" he asked.

"Disparage my husband. I really loved him, and still miss him," she mumbled.

He stroked her face. "I didn't mean to be disparaging. At least you had the courage to try commitment. I sure as hell never did."

"Is this a good idea?" she asked.

Shrugging again he replied, "I don't know. We'll see."

"That's a major endorsement," she complained.

"It's the truth. Neither of us knows. Though I would think I'd get some points for moving in here with you."

Sara kissed him gently, but with passion. "You do. It was very gutsy."

"Time to get up," said Michael, swinging his legs over the edge of the bed. "What do you want for lunch?"

"He cooks too!" she exclaimed, though of course she already knew that. "Whatever you're making."

"I didn't say I was going to make it," he deadpanned as he struggled into his jeans. "I wanted to know what you were going to make."

"Ha-ha-ha," she grumbled. "I think I want a BLT sandwich on rye."

"Sounds good to me," he said, already headed for the kitchen.

"Bacon's in the cheese drawer," she called after him.

"Found it."

Tingle

Sara decided to luxuriate for a few minutes before jumping into the shower. By the time she headed out to the kitchen, she could smell the bacon, which was sizzling on the grill in the center of her stove. Michael grinned at her. "Tomatoes are already cut and ready, and the bread's toasting." Sara's tummy clenched. 'Bread's toasting' was what Jeffrey always said when he had made their BLT sandwiches. She wished she hadn't thought of that, but then decided it might just mean she had a good picker, in terms of the two most significant men in her life.

"I like it when your hair's wet and curls up like that," he said, something else that reminded her of her dead husband.

She changed the subject immediately. "How about driving out to the Pine Barrens today and taking a hike?" she asked him.

"That sounds great. I've never been to the Pine Barrens, though I have friends who hike there," he turned, a look of excitement on his face.

"What shoes do you have here?" she asked, since his feet were still bare and she didn't remember what he'd unpacked.

"Tennis shoes. Nikes. I presume that'll be OK," he said.

"Yup. No problem," she sat and tucked into the sandwich he had set down on the table. "Yum."

"It was your idea," he turned from the oven, grinning at her.

"I used to eat these with my father," she said with her mouth full.

"My mom has always told me talking with your mouth full was rude!"

When Sara gave him the finger, taking an enormous bite, his laugh was deep, and very appealing. She wondered if she loved him, but the thought was a bit overwhelming so she just smiled and kept eating.

"I made four sandwiches, since I figured you'd be hungry," he explained as he, too, sat down with a full plate.

"Braggart!"

She finished first, watching him inhale his first sandwich and begin on the second. "How do you stay so slim?" she asked.

"Working out. Every day."

"You're talking with your mouth full," she teased, but all he did was shrug. He didn't tell her he wasn't sure he would be able to finish the second sandwich.

"I'm gonna get out my Jersey maps and figure out the best route to the Pine Barrens. I don't really remember," she explained as she left the kitchen.

"Your turn to clean up," he called after her.

"Too bad," she called back. Then she reappeared. "We may have to stay over someplace. It takes several hours to drive there...."

"Good thing it's not in the South then," he replied, deadpan.

"You don't think we'll have a problem?" she asked. "I wish that didn't worry me, but it does."

"One of us can stay in the car while the other goes in to pay, probably you. I don't mean to be paranoid either, but better safe than sorry I figure," Michael replied. Then he shrugged again, a gesture that was becoming quite familiar. "We'll have to get up really early tomorrow so I can get to the library on time," he added as he went to the bedroom to retrieve a pair of jeans and a sweater.

When he returned, fully clothed, Sara had already thrown apples, oranges and bananas into the cooler at her feet. "How about trail mix?" he asked her. She held up a baggie, fully stuffed, dropping it in as well, then adding some sodas and coconut water before slamming it shut.

Tingle

"I guess you have a car," he grunted as he hefted the thing into his arms, adding, "I hope it's close."

"In the basement. Follow me," she said, leading the way.

Once they were on the road, she started to talk about her regrets at putting off the decision to have children. "We thought we had time," she explained.

When he raised his eyebrows, she knew what he was asking and continued. "Jeffrey wanted children more than I did, and agreed to wait."

"There was no way you could have known," he told her.

"It was still a mistake. Back then I thought I wanted to have a career in publishing," she explained. He quickly turned his head to her in surprise. "Yes, I worked at Simon and Schuster in the art department, but I sure didn't think it was in exchange for kids. Then he got sick," she trailed off.

"We're a little old," he muttered.

"Oh Michael, that's not what I meant," she laid a hand on his leg. Michael was driving, delighted to have his hands on the wheel and a chance to drive, which he didn't have very often.

"I'm surprised I said that," he replied. "If we were a little younger…even with the obvious problems…" his voice trailed off.

"It's OK," she reassured him. "I don't think I could handle being a mother at this late date."

"I didn't think I'd ever even consider parenthood," he agreed.

"Whatever it is we're doing sure has had all sorts of surprises, at least for me," she sighed.

"Me too."

They drove along, content, neither feeling as if they had to make conversation. Once they had reached the Garden State Parkway in

New Jersey, the scenery they were passing became more beautiful, rural and rich with color and both were happy to just stare and pursue their own thoughts.

"Maybe we should get married," Michael said, interrupting Sara's reverie about the countryside. Had she been standing up, she might have keeled over. "Wow," he said, glancing at her face. "That's a hell of a response!"

"I'm just shocked, is all," she explained as she took a very deep breath. "We're beyond having kids, as we've both just admitted, so why?" she asked. After all, he had already finished moving all of his things over to her condo.

"Because neither of us has ever felt this way before. Because we love each other," he continued.

'We do?' she thought. Neither had actually uttered those words.

"And I guess because this is what I was always told a good marriage felt like," he finished his thought.

"By whom?" she asked.

"My aunt. She was not referring to my parents' marriage, and not really her own, though it was a hell of a lot better than my mom's. Her sister," he added in explanation.

Sara shrugged, lips pursed. Then she teased, "Including the blow jobs?"

Michael responded with a grin. "My Aunt didn't talk about that. Hey, did you ever think that maybe we both taste so sweet because of our healthy eating habits. And I know you're changing the subject."

Sara wondered if he wanted a real marriage, or just a commitment ceremony, and who would attend. She asked, and was pleased that he preferred a commitment ceremony. Wow, were they really thinking about doing that too? She agreed to look for a place, maybe in the

Tingle

Catskills, or someplace closer to the City than the Pine Barrens so their friends could get there easily. She did suggest they wait a couple of months. Maybe she could find a place close to a train line.

Michael agreed the wait was a good idea, 'to see how they did with living together', which was a relief to Sarah. One step at a time is what she thought.

They relished their hike on one of the trails through the many acres of wilderness in southern Jersey and returned to the City, both comfortable with their earlier discussion and the decision they appeared to have made. They returned to their regular lives, Michael at the library and Sara at their condo, with her friends, and working apace on the outline for her novel because of his encouragement.

Chapter 5

When Michael came home on Friday evening, as soon as he walked in the door Sara blurted, "I invited Jordan and Lucy for dinner on Saturday. I thought it would be good for one set of our friends to see us together and get to know the 'us' of us!" She was breathless by the time she finished these few sentences.

A bit surprised, Michael nevertheless told her the invitation seemed a good idea to him. Later they made their dinner salad side by side, and it wasn't until they were sitting at the table with the pot roast and prune dish Sara had made earlier in the day that she was calm enough to say, "If you want to invite Jevon and his lady friend too," she began, but couldn't go on because Michael burst out laughing.

"Lady friend? God, I haven't heard that phrase since I was in high school. And the only guys who used it were white, or very very square!"

"Don't be a bigot," she said, and then started to laugh too. "What do you call someone you're living with but not married to?" she asked.

"I don't know. Your partner?" he replied.

"That's good. I like that. But maybe other people will think you're using that word to protect them because your significant other is the same sex," she wondered aloud.

Michael just shrugged, as if to say, 'So what?'

"Sometimes I say very silly things," she mumbled.

"Yup," Michael agreed, mouth full of the yams that had been roasting with the meat all afternoon.

"God, I love this dish," he added after he had swallowed.

They ate in companionable silence for a few minutes. Then Michael said, "Let's do one couple at a time. Then if we think they'll hit it off we can decide we want to have them over together."

"Good idea. And I hope they do cause I've always loved having dinner parties," she explained.

"I've always been more private," he began.

"No kidding!" she interrupted. They smiled at one another, neither discomfited by the discussion.

"So what are we making?" he asked as he cut himself another slice of the pot roast.

"I thought we could barbecue steaks, make a big salad, and maybe do some stir-fry potatoes," she suggested. "But I didn't buy anything 'cause I thought we should plan our menu together."

Michael nodded, saying, "That sounds like a good dinner to me. We can get bread at Amy's."

"Yum!" Sara's eyes glowed.

"Yum?" he teased.

Tingle

"Oh yeah. I can picture you cutting it lengthwise and slathering it with melted butter and garlic!"

"Yum!" he agreed, grinning his wonderful infectious grin. "What about dessert?"

"How about my chocolate buttermilk cake?"

"That sounds great. How come you've never made it for me?" he complained, though not seriously.

This time Sara shrugged. "We hardly ever eat dessert. By the time we finish our meal and clean up, you're dragging me into the bedroom."

Michael laughed aloud, managing to sputter, "I've never heard you complain."

With a very serious expression, Sara asked, "Should we head there now or do the dishes first?"

More laughter, but they did clean up first, and then watched Rachel Maddow before repairing to the boudoir. As Sara began to strip off her jeans, Michael stopped her saying, "Let me" which she did. It still felt delicious to sense his fingers on the waistband as he unbuttoned, unzipped, and then began to draw them down her hips, past her knees, and to the floor. She hoped it would feel that way for years, lasting well into their seventies, though that felt a long way off. She knew from Marty's mom that it was closer than any of them believed, but she had never dared to ask the seventy-four year old if she and Marty's father still 'indulged' and enjoyed that part of their life together.

Michael called in the middle of the day to say he would be late coming home. He had something to do.

When he crawled into bed next to her, he rolled her into his arms and said, "I went to see my mom in Newark."

"You did?" Sara squealed.

"It took her awhile to accept that I was living with a white woman, and by the time she did – 'If you love her and she is good to you' she finally said – accepting that I had actually asked you to marry me wasn't that big a stretch."

Sara was so stunned by the information, for once she was speechless.

"She does want to meet you. I thought I could go out get her and bring her here for dinner one night," Michael continued.

"Wow," that feels scary. Can we wait until we've seen how our best friends react to us?" she asked, knowing she was just trying to postpone the inevitable.

Michael stroked her face. "That's exactly what I told her I wanted to do, which made sense to her," he said.

The next morning after she had finished four pages of her novel, Sara called Lucy, who would be on the way home from her Nia class, to extend the first invite.

"What a great idea. We'd love to come to dinner Saturday," Lucy declared with delight.

"You haven't even asked Jordan," Sara replied with a chuckle.

"If he has any plans already, I'll eat my hat!" her friend stated with vigor. Then she added, "And if he does, he can change them."

Sara and Michael bought the steaks together on Saturday morning, lingering over the salad section at the market, choosing the perfect tomatoes and radishes, and mildly arguing over spring mix versus baby romaine. They settled on the spring mix, as well as mini organic carrots, red onion and a can of black olives. When Sara grabbed a pippin apple, Michael didn't utter a word. He didn't have to eat it; he could push it aside or eat around it. Much to his surprise that evening he actually found he liked the taste.

Tingle

They returned to the condo and decided to clean, which didn't take very long since Sara had scrubbed the place the preceding Tuesday. They stripped their sheets and threw them in the laundry, finally settling down in the tiny yard on their respective lounges, each with a popular mystery. It amused her that Michael had known which authors to suggest to her because he loved reading mysteries too, something she never would have guessed. He seemed much too erudite for such guilty pleasures. They went inside in the late afternoon to shower, set the table, and make the salad together, as usual standing side by side at the kitchen counter, chatting about the news, which they were listening to on the kitchen radio. WBAI, of course.

Lucy arrived bearing a welcome gift, Jordan carrying the huge bouquet of flowers they had bought at Gabriela Wakeham. Lucy deposited the huge platter of homemade hors d'oevres. Just looking at them made Michael's mouth water – "She makes the best ones!" Sara declared, grabbing a shrimp and cream cheese before the platter even reached the kitchen counter.

"Jeez, when did you become so greedy?" Jordan asked her with a smile.

"I think when I was about eight," Sara replied after giving his question mock and obvious thought. Michael watched the banter with bemusement: his mom hadn't been able to afford such things; making sure they had enough food for school lunches and supper had been both his concern and experience. He had never eaten pre-dinner snacks, even as an adult, but he had to admit they looked delicious, at least some of them. When Sara grabbed another from the platter and told him to open his mouth, he immediately complied.

"Wow, what is that?" he turned to Lucy to ask. "It's great!"

"Prosciutto and a special cheese I always buy. I dunk the whole thing in olive oil and then put it on a Triscuit," she told him, grabbing one for herself. "They're my favorites."

Sara seized the bottle of chardonnay that had been chilling in the refrigerator, and they all headed into the living room.

"Those steaks looked great. Who else is coming for dinner?" Jordan asked. He meant it: the New York steaks were huge; one for each of them.

"That's what I asked when Sara picked them out," Michael agreed. "She told me leftover steak not only makes great sandwiches, but is even better on top of a salad, knowing how much I love greens."

"So how long have you been a librarian?" Jordan asked as he popped another one of his wife's concoctions into his mouth.

"Fifteen years," he replied, startled to realize it was the same amount of time that Sara had been married to Jeffrey.

"How time flies," Sara grinned. "I had no idea you'd been suggesting books to me for so long."

"And certainly no idea I'd be suggesting other things as well," Michael quipped, wondering if he was crossing a line. When both Lucy and her husband laughed, he glanced at Sara who was grinning too, and began to relax. Maybe he would actually enjoy the evening.

"Do you guys want to put the steaks on?" Lucy asked, still chewing on a cracker topped with her special cheese.

"Very chauvinistic of you, I'd say," Jordan groused.

"You beat me to it," said Michael.

The two men smiled at each other as they rose and headed for the kitchen.

Tingle

Sara called after them, "I lit the grill just before you got here. So it's already hot." She paused and told Lucy, "I have no idea if either of them heard me."

"Doesn't matter, unless one of them decides to test it by touching the grate," Lucy replied. "I really like him."

"Me too," Sara smiled. "Do you think Jordan does?"

"Are you kidding? I've never seen him as happy to go out to barbecue steak before," she replied, reaching over to squeeze her friend's hand. They both sipped their chardonnay.

Almost in a whisper, Sara murmured, "He asked me to marry him."

"Wow! I think that's great. Were you surprised?" Lucy asked her.

"Yeah, I was surprised. We've just started living together," Sara replied.

"Sweetie, just take a deep breath and be grateful you can love again. Can you do that?" Lucy asked.

"I don't know why I'm having such a hard time," Sara muttered. She couldn't believe it when Lucy said, "Jeffrey would want you to be happy. He would want this for you."

"Oh God," was all Sara could say.

"You know he'd like him," Lucy suggested.

"Yes, I've even thought that a few times, but it doesn't seem to help me," Sara sighed, sick unto death of sighing.

Lucy leaned over and took both of Sara's hands in hers. "They'll be back any minute. Breathe. We'll talk tomorrow. Think grateful thoughts tonight when you go to sleep. Look at him lying next to you, and realize how amazing it is that you've found him."

Before Sara could reply, they heard the sliding door to the tiny yard open, and then the voices of the men. Jordan was talking about his work; he was an account executive at a small publishing company that specialized in boutique-type magazines.

"See," Lucy squeezed Sara's hands as she let go. "He never talks about his work to anyone. He's gonna have a male friend. How fabulous."

Sara was stunned. She hadn't let herself hope the evening would be successful, let alone this successful. Since her invitation she hadn't let herself wonder if they would get along, or not. She wasn't sure if it was scarier that they both really liked him, or that she had been afraid that they wouldn't. Lucy and Jordan didn't leave until well after midnight, despite the fact that Michael had to be at work by 9 because he was covering someone else's shift. When the door closed behind them, he patted Sara's buns, saying, "Don't look at me like that. At least you can sleep in."

They fell into each other's arms in the hallway before they even reached their bedroom, leaving a trail of clothes behind them, which amused Michael when he raced off to the library in the morning.

He had taken his time making love to this who woman he still couldn't believe had become the central focus of his life. He really couldn't imagine doing anything without her, or at least without her waiting for him at home. He started with her nipples, rubbing them through the silk of her blouse, lowering the blouse from her shoulders but continuing to stroke the nipples with his graceful fingers.

"Aren't you tired," she moaned, not asking him to stop.

"No more than you. Maybe I should just slip inside for a quickie," he said, eyes smiling down at hers.

"No you don't. I'm gonna come any second and then I'll take care of you," she managed and then was crying out. "Don't you dare say I don't have to; just give me a minute."

Tingle

"You can take as long as you want, my love. I feel quite content." He lay beside her with a lovely smile on his face, as if to prove the point.

He almost fell asleep while she was licking his erect cock, but not quite. She had a real talent for the job, which he told her afterwards before he did drift off.

The next day Sara realized she had finished reading the library books Michael had brought home for her in the beginning of the month and decided to surprise him by bringing them back herself. Besides, she had gotten stuck in her own novel – maybe outlining would have been a good idea – so walking over there seemed a welcome relief. He didn't see her when she entered the lobby because he was talking to another customer, a good-looking woman, she noticed. She was surprised at how much it bothered her to see him conversing with a woman she thought better looking than herself, so she stayed by the entryway, only walking over to his desk once the 'other' woman had walked away. Michael was jotting down notes on the pad he kept, probably to help him remember which of his clients read which books – that's how he remembers! she thought – so he didn't notice her at all. When she put the books down on the desk, near the pad he was writing on, he looked up.

His response was immediate and marvelous. He smiled at her with his entire face. "Well, hello you! This is a treat. I didn't expect to see you for another six hours!"

"I didn't realize how much fun it would be to surprise you," she smiled back at him.

They stood there grinning at each other, not even noticing a few library patrons pass by and glance their way because of the intensity of their expressions and how happy they both looked.

Then Sara explained, "I finished all of these; my novel is refusing to budge; and I didn't feel like going to the gym, so here I am."

"I sure am happy to see you, as you can probably tell. I could probably take a fifteen-minute break. Want to go for coffee?" he asked.

"Sure. It's a little early in the day for wine," she replied.

"Though you wouldn't mind having a glass, I bet. Loosen up those writing juices."

"Just seeing you helps. I already have a few sentences in my head." She took a pad from her purse and jotted them down as he walked over to the young man who was working in the library stacking books. By the time they both returned, she was ready to go as well.

"Take a half hour, Michael," the boy called after them. "I don't have any more books to stack now anyway."

The both ordered decaf latte's, and then Michael called after the waitress, "And a chocolate croissant, please."

Sara groaned. "A plain one would have been bad enough."

"You don't need to have any," he shrugged.

"I may have to rethink this whole thing. I didn't know you were mean," she groused.

When their order arrived, Sara was the first one to tear off a piece of the flakey pastry, rolling it around in her mouth before swallowing.

"I can see the wattles growing on your upper arms," Michael said, totally deadpan.

"I'll change the locks before you come home tonight. Your clothes will be out in the hall," she mumbled around her second bite of croissant.

The next day Michael called Jevon at work and invited him and Margery to dinner the following Saturday. Jevon called back to

Tingle

see if they could come on Sunday instead of Saturday, because his significant other had already made plans with one of her friends for a Saturday dinner date. Sara and Michael did their food shopping Saturday and were able to relax most of the day on Sunday, making the salad in the late afternoon, again side by side. They had again bought steaks, deciding they would be equal opportunity weekend dinner hosts.

Jevon was clearly uncomfortable as they showed them around the condo, though Margery was excited by the light blue color they had chosen for the bedroom, especially the dark blue accent wall behind the bed.

"I think I would have wanted this blue in front of me so I could see it, or to the side," she said, eyes aglow with excitement.

"Next she's gonna say she wants to do this in our bedroom," Jevon complained to the room at large.

"I promise," began Sara, "It won't take as long as you think it will."

"She's teasing you, Jevon, but it's true," Michael said.

Margery turned to him, an expectant look on her face.

"If we're going to do this, I think we should do it in the living room," Jevon suggested. Margery was thrilled.

"This has been terrific and we haven't even eaten anything yet," Margery declared.

"Then come into the kitchen, my dear, so we can remedy that," Michael suggested with his hand on her back to guide her. "Sara got a really great appetizer recipe from a friend of hers and thought we should try it out on you guys."

As he trailed behind them Jevon still seemed uncomfortable. "I know you don't think we should get married so soon," Sara began but Jevon raised his hand.

"Probably. But look how long I've been living with Margery without even mentioning the word," he turned to her with a smile.

Sara wouldn't be deterred. "You sure that's the only reason?"

"I've never seen Michael this relaxed, or I guess the right word is happy," he replied, not sounding very convincing.

"But I'm white," Sara said with her usual directness.

That actually made him laugh, not a belly laugh, but a laugh nonetheless. "You aren't like any white person I've ever met!"

She actually smiled. "That's something my husband, Jeffrey always said, except he substituted the word 'woman' for 'white'".

At that Jevon turned to appraise her. "Hmmm. Maybe that's why you've turned his head around. Smart, direct, and very female." He didn't pause for long. "And did I say pretty too?"

Sara was embarrassed. "Thank you," she said quietly. "I won't try to change him. I promise. At least not any more than any woman tries to change her man."

At that, Jevon linked his arm through hers. "OK. You win. I accept this is happening for my oldest friend. Hell, after I see how it goes, maybe I'll follow in your footsteps."

"And how long will that take? Seeing how this goes?" she teased.

"Jesus. You sound like Margery, and she's known me a very long time," he groused.

Chapter 6

Because Sarah had way more free time, the task of finding a place for their wedding ceremony fell to her. It was a job she realized she liked. Using the internet she found pictures of several of the small resorts she thought would suit them, which made the search quite enjoyable. Finally she settled upon a place in the Pine Barrens, only seventy-nine miles from the City. It was a rustic inn with twelve cabins and a main building with a dining hall and room for a dance floor. The web site even listed several local bands with different specialties. Blues/jazz seemed to fit their musical tastes, so she sent off an email to see if the band was free on any of the dates they were considering. Best of all, the lead cabin had a hot tub outside the bedroom on the porch, which she thought would be marvelous in the crisp fall weather. When Michael came home from work the day she discovered the place, she excitedly called him over to her desk, the website pictures already up on the screen.

Michael waxed profound, going from picture to picture more than once, kidding that he had heard that hot tubs made erections more difficult to achieve. "Not worried about that at all," Sara announced, looking over his shoulder. He was sitting at her desk chair to better peruse the site. Her arms were crossed over his chest, face close to his, so she began to nibble on his ear lobe.

Within seconds they had stumbled to their bed, a fairly easy move since the desk was set up in the bedroom, and fell upon the mattress, reaching for buttons, zippers, shoes and socks. If anything, their passion for one another had increased rather than decreased over the short course of their burgeoning relationship. Each was finding new ways to please the other: when Michael used his tongue around the opening to her vagina, Sara almost lost her mind, coming within seconds. This of course pleased him no end, and helped fuel his desire to find new tricks to try. Sara was equally inventive. And so their lovemaking became more exciting, a reality neither of them expected or imagined.

For a few days Michael seemed to have forgotten about the resort. At least he didn't look at it again, or ask Sara if she thought they had made the right choice. She was relieved despite having found the place, because even now she wasn't positive she actually wanted to marry again. They had told their best friends: she didn't admit her prevaricating to anyone, especially since he had even told his mother. Marrying again still somehow seemed disrespectful to Jeffrey, or his memory, or the memory of the married life they had shared for so many years. And then at dinner one night, Michael took her hand and brought it to his lips.

Tingle

"Have you called the resort and booked it yet?" he asked, his anxiety about bringing up the subject apparent.

Sara sighed. "Oh Michael. I still have such mixed feelings about getting married again. But I haven't known how to talk to you about them."

"Why don't you just begin," he calmly suggested, though his stomach was churning.

Another sigh. "I've been thinking a lot about my marriage to Jeffrey."

When she again paused, Michael quietly said, "That's not surprising."

Sara sniffled, rubbing the top of her hand under her nose. Michael waited, but this time he didn't seem particularly patient.

"It almost feels like disrespecting what we had, to consider trying marriage with someone else," she whispered, finally voicing aloud what she had been thinking.

"Not just someone else. Me. The man you love," he responded.

Again she sighed. 'I know. That's what makes this so hard."

"You're going to change your mind," he said, voice shaking.

"I didn't say that. I just need more time to figure out everything I'm feeling," she returned.

He actually looked angry. She had never seen his face take on that expression, and it both frightened and upset her. "Please," she said. "Please give me a little more time to digest everything."

"Is it because…"he began but Sara interrupted.

"Don't go there. That's your issue, not mine."

This time she, too, sounded angry. They had never fought about anything before.

"Then why?" he demanded.

"I need to make peace with abandoning Jeffrey," she muttered.

"How the hell are you abandoning him? He's dead," Michael asked, incredulous.

"It doesn't make sense, I know. But that's how it feels to me," she replied.

"What about what we've been doing together. The way you come. The way I come. Does that disrespect him?" he asked, not comprehending at all.

"It's the idea of marriage. It's so final."

When he pushed away from the table abruptly, knocking over his chair, and grabbed his jacket from the hook by the front door, stalking out without another word, Sara was too shocked to stop him. Then she, too, opened the door, but he was gone.

It was finding no trace of him on the stairs, or even in the street, that brought her to tears. She felt totally trapped, unable to say 'yes' but equally unwilling to lose him. She picked up her phone and called his cell, but he didn't answer. Next she called Lucy, who wasn't answering either. Then Sara remembered Lucy had her Spanish class on Thursday nights. She had no idea when the class adjourned. Instead of going upstairs to her bed, Sara dropped onto her kitchen chair, slumping and resting her head on the table, still crying. She didn't think she'd ever be able to stop.

She tried calling Michael several times over the next few hours until she fell asleep, and then in desperation walked over to the library in the morning. As soon as he saw her, he disappeared into the office. She stood there waiting but he didn't come back out, so she left.

What could she do if he wouldn't even talk to her?

Her friend wasn't actually moving into his apartment until the end of the month, so she decided she would go there when she knew

Tingle

he would be in for the evening. A neighbor let her into the building when Michael didn't answer his buzzer. When she kept knocking on his apartment door, he finally opened it. He looked awful, and had obviously been crying, his eyes red and puffy. Sighing, he moved aside so she could step inside.

Sarah started crying again. "Please talk to me, Michael," she whispered.

At first he didn't say anything, but when she looked up and realized he was again crying, she moved towards him, holding out her arms. His body remained stiff, but he did put his arms around her shoulders.

"Maybe we should take a break so we can both figure out what we want here, and then talk and decide if it's the same thing," he said through his tears.

"It isn't that I don't love you," Sara began.

"I know that. I do. But you're not sure you want to marry me, and I don't think I can handle that and go on with this, whatever this is," he told her.

She mumbled into his shoulder, "How long should this 'break' be?"

She could feel him shrug. "I don't know. Maybe a month," he replied, which made her cry all the harder.

"I can't imagine not seeing you for a month," she said, again whispering.

"I don't know how to deal with you pulling back, but I think we have to take a break so we can figure out what we want without trying to influence each other," he explained.

They stayed, standing together, his arms around her, Sara trying to move closer. But that wasn't the problem; it was the stiffness of his body, which she had never felt before. Finally she stepped back and turned, opening the door, and taking the stairs down two flights because she didn't want to wait for the elevator. By the time she was almost back to her condo, Lucy called.

"Stop sobbing and come over. Where are you?" she asked.

"Almost home. I guess I can walk over to your place," Sara said, taking a deep, heaving breath as she replied.

Lucy held her for a long time, until Sara could stop crying. "Tell me," she said and Sara did, in halting phrases, and with difficulty.

"Jeffrey would want you to be happy," Lucy gently reminded her.

"I know that, but…" again a big sigh. "It's just that marrying again seems…so disrespectful."

"Why isn't the sex disrespectful?" Lucy asked her, despite knowing that the question might feel too intrusive given Sara's condition.

At first Sara didn't respond, and then she said, "I'm not sure. Maybe because I told myself I was having an affair and it was just about sex, so it didn't relate at all to what I had with Jeffrey."

"No, it didn't," her friend agreed. "And it wouldn't if you married him either."

"Why" Sara asked her, feeling ridiculous.

"Because the relationships are totally different. You and Jeffrey were kids when you married, and you grew together over many years. That intimacy can never be challenged, no matter what you do or don't do with Michael," Lucy replied.

"I didn't feel guilty when we were just screwing," Sara mumbled, but Lucy interrupted.

"You weren't just screwing, Sara."

"But I could pretend, at least at first, that that's what we were doing. And I've always been so square, I'd never done that before, so it kind of seemed OK."

Tingle

"But his proposal brought it all out into the open. You're not just having sex with this man, you love him too," Lucy shook her head in agreement.

"Oh God," Sara moaned. 'I do, but I also don't know if I can marry him, and I don't understand why."

"Michael's right. You need to think about it," Lucy said, sighing as well. "And I also understand why he is so upset. I really do. And since you can't tell him, or me for that matter, why – this is in your court, honey," she told Sara, stroking her back.

"OK," Sara sighed. "It must be really late. I should go home."

"Why don't you make dinner for us tomorrow after you've had some time to think, and we can talk some more," Lucy suggested.

As she was making a beef stew for their dinner the following night, Sara couldn't help thinking that she had bought the ingredients before Michael had stormed out of the condo the day before and had planned on making this dinner for them. He had once told her that stew was one of his favorite meals, proving forever that he was a peasant at heart no matter how many degrees he had managed to collect.

"You are much too intelligent and astute for a peasant," she had told him with a laugh, adding, "to say nothing of elegant."

He, too, had laughed, protesting that the last trait was learned, even if he had been born with the first two.

Why had she never told him she loved him? Why did the very idea of marrying him terrify her? Underneath her liberal exterior, was she conventional? Having an affair with a black man was fine, marrying him something else entirely? She had no answer for any of her questions, and didn't really find any by talking with Lucy later that evening.

"Even when he asked me to marry him, neither of us had ever said 'I love you'", she told Lucy. "He hadn't either."

"Do you think he loves you?" her friend asked. And then, "Do you love him?"

Sara sighed. She had been sighing all day long. "Yes and yes. But at our age, we don't have to marry the people we love," she added, sounding lame even to herself.

Lucy grabbed her hand. "You've always said you believed in marriage!"

Sigh. "I did. I do."

"But?" came the obvious question.

"We haven't known each other that long," Sara mumbled. "Lame."

"Yeah, it is. I haven't seen you this happy in a long time, even before Jeffrey died," Lucy said.

"Well, he was sick for a long time, and I sure wasn't happy then," Sara declared, annoyed. Had she ever felt this kind of excitement with her husband? She didn't remember. At the beginning, maybe. But they had both been so innocent, sexually, that the passion hadn't been as free at first, and then their love-making had more to do with expressing the depth of their feelings for one another rather than the heat they might have felt in one another's presence.

Lucy waited for Sara to finish talking about her confused thoughts and feelings. When she had, Lucy suggested, "It's never the same, person to person. You haven't had much experience with many men, to say the least, so you'll just have to trust me on this."

"Is what Michael and I have been experiencing unusual?" she asked her friend.

This time Lucy sighed. "Yes."

Tingle

"Have you ever…" Sara started to ask, wondering if she should, because suddenly Lucy looked sad.

"Not in many years, sweetie," she said. "I think you should think long and hard before you throw it away."

Irritated, Sara blurted, "I'm not throwing it away. I think I was the one who suggested he move in; I'm just not sure I can marry him."

"Ever?" Lucy asked. "Don't cry, Sarie," she urged, using her college nickname for her old friend. "I know it's not fun, but you really need to be thinking this through."

Lucy left by midnight, accepting the twenty-dollar bill Sara shoved in her hand for the cab ride home. They both knew she was nervous about taking the subway alone at such a late hour. Sara felt better, though she didn't understand her reticence about moving forward with Michael's proposal any more than she had before her long heart-to-heart with her oldest friend. But she fell asleep right away because she was utterly exhausted. In the morning she kept wiping the tears away as she ate her bagel, and had to hold herself back from walking over to the library again. Though she did wonder if she went every day, would Michael realize how much she loved him, and how confused she felt?

No. She had to honor his need for time to think things through: a whole month. She wondered what he would do about his apartment. He certainly couldn't stay with her friend while they took the break he believed was so essential.

. . . .

Michael had never been a man who cried easily. He was too careful for that. But the first few nights he slept in his old bed, which Sara's friend was going to use, he couldn't seem to stop. He missed her more than he had even expected, the warmth of her body next to his, the funny little noises she made as she slept, the sounds of her stumbling to the bathroom and back in the middle of the night. And the love making. Because that's what it had been after the first few times. He just hadn't realized, or hadn't wanted to admit it to himself, let along to Sara. If it was about love, good Lord, what would that mean?

He knew he should have told her, maybe not that quickly, but certainly sometime in the last few months, that he loved her. Maybe if he had, she wouldn't have been so shocked by his proposal.

Hell, he had been shocked, even though he had been thinking about marrying her for the last month, and even longer. He hadn't made a decision to ask her, the words had just come bursting forth. That lovely afternoon, holding her hand to help her over a large boulder and then just hanging on to it, sharing sandwiches, and eating from the same apple, everything about the day had felt so right that he had known he had to take the next step.

"You asshole," he told himself. "You didn't even give her a hint."

But he couldn't make himself call her, or apologize, or change the boundaries he had set, even if he now saw them as precipitous.

Her hesitation must have had something to do with the differences between them. 'Differences, my ass,' he thought. 'With my being black.'

His distrust of white people was part of his psyche, which was why he had hesitated about getting involved with her in the first place. He had liked her a lot for some time, thoroughly enjoying their discussions about books. The fact that looking at her was very pleasant hadn't hurt either. The first time he had put his hand on her arm, the shock that went through him had been unnerving. That jolt hadn't been momentary; it had lasted long after she had left the library.

Tingle

Michael had never mourned anyone, so he didn't really understand the depth of his sadness. Finally he looked up grief in his little pocket dictionary, and there it was: he had passed the first stage, denial, and was well into the second. He just didn't really know who to be angry at: Sara? Of course, he decided. She shouldn't need to think about his proposal. Even if he hadn't given her any kind of warning, moving his belongings over to her condo should have been a sign of something! His precious private belongings. That action implied love to him, even if he hadn't said the actual word, even to himself. He certainly couldn't admit he was being ridiculous.

He ran into his neighbor, Cheryl, in the hallway one evening when he was returning to his apartment with a pizza. Pizza? He never ate pizza. She looked at him, and said, "You better come in for a glass of wine." He didn't want to talk to anyone, let alone his intrusive neighbor, but he didn't know how to say no. She was just being kind.

As she handed him a glass of very fine merlot, she asked, "So what happened?"

"With what?" he replied, knowing how silly that must have sounded.

"Michael…!" was all she said in return.

"I proposed," he admitted. If his skin could have turned pink, it would have.

"Wow," she gasped, clearly surprised.

"Yeah, I was too. Surprised I mean," he admitted.

"She said no?" Cheryl asked him, incredulous.

"No. She said she needed time to think about it. To digest the idea, I think was what she said," he replied. "Of course she didn't say no either."

Cheryl raised her hands in a 'so?' gesture.

Michael took a deep breath. "I stormed out so I can't go back."

"Of course you can if you love her," Cheryl disagreed, totally surprised by her own response. After all, Sara was white, and she thoroughly disapproved of black men dating white women, let alone marrying one.

"I do, but I still can't." he said.

"Why?" she asked him again.

"I don't know," he muttered. He had no idea that the woman he loved was having the same struggle.

"Is it because she's white?" Cheryl posed the question, wondering if she was asking because of her own prejudice. She never had used that word before about her own beliefs, just about white beliefs.

"No, I don't think so. I've never even lived with anyone before, so popping the question was such a big deal, she should have known."

Cheryl laughed. "You sound like a fifth grader."

"Ha ha ha. I feel like one," Michael had to admit.

"You sure look sad," she said. "And though I hate to admit it, you bastard, for never even looking at me, the one time I talked with her I actually liked the woman."

That made Michael smile. "She's very likeable. As for you, you were my neighbor. If we had had a go at each other and it didn't work, I would have had to move."

"Had a go…? Where do you come from?" she laughed again. "Here, have another glass of wine and sip this time so you can taste it. It's really good stuff."

"Taste?" he joked, "What's that?" as he took a sip. His eyebrows arched. "It is good."

"Michael, I think you really have to think about this. You could be making the biggest mistake of your life, such as it is," she suggested.

Tingle

"I think maybe I have to go out on some dates, to clear my mind," he countered.

"To get laid, you mean," she said, annoyed.

He merely shrugged. "That's not a bad idea either."

His neighbor had heard enough. "Maybe this is why I've stayed single all these years. Men are…"

"Pigs," he interrupted. "Look," he tried to explain. "If I'm going to figure out whether what we have is special enough to accept that we may just live together without going further, I may have to compare, to see if it is as special as I've thought it was…."

Amazed, she demanded, "The feelings you've been talking about aren't enough?"

"They are and they're not, I guess," he replied slowly, embarrassed, but unwilling to say he wasn't going to try a few dates anyway.

Back in his own small apartment he suddenly could picture a black woman with smooth skin the color of cocoa, cooked cocoa steaming in a big ceramic cup, but couldn't remember where he had seen her. It wasn't until he was toweling off in his bathroom that it came to him: she was a checker at the Whole Foods on 7th Avenue where he frequently shopped. He needed a few things, and decided to shop for them on his way home from the library the next day.

He was disappointed that she wasn't standing at her usual check stand, which was empty. 'Oh well, maybe that's a message,' he thought. But he still had to shop, and wandered the aisles looking for things he might need, given that he would be feeding himself for a whole month. To heighten his discomfort, he had to admit he had grown used to Sara's cooking. She was inventive and creative in the masterpieces that appeared on their table almost every night. She cooked as she lived. God, he really missed her.

Nancy Alvarez

As he rolled his cart towards the checkout stands, he realized the woman he had been thinking about was in her usual place. Without another thought of Sara, he rolled his cart to the appropriate line, although it was longer than any of the others. Maybe Cheryl was right about men.

"Haven't seen you in awhile," she said with a huge smile as he began to unload his fairly full cart. Michael wondered what he was going to do with all the stuff he was putting on the counter. Most of it would spoil before he could eat it. He hesitated, thinking 'I've been with Sara,' but actually saying, "I've been busy. Eating out a lot."

Why was he lying? He never lied. He didn't have to say where he was eating; being busy would have sufficed.

"Lucky you," she said as she began to ring up his groceries.

"Do you ever eat out when you get off?" he asked, as surprised by the words coming out of his mouth as he had been by his marriage proposal.

She grinned. "Depends who I'm eating with."

"What are you doing tonight?" he asked.

"But you have all this food," she replied, enjoying the flirtation.

"It'll keep. When do you get off?" he asked, not backing down.

"Seven," she said. "A little late for dinner."

"In New York?" he asked, voice raised in mock shock. Most of his friends didn't sit down to eat dinner until at least 9.

Shrugging, she said, "Sure. Why not?"

"I'll be waiting outside. I guess you're not married," he stated as an afterthought.

"Nope. Never had the courage to even live with anyone," she agreed.

"Me neither," he said, thinking 'until a few months ago', which of course he didn't say.

Tingle

He quickly walked away with two full bags in his arms. Both of them were embarrassed, neither expecting what had just occurred.

Guilt overwhelmed him as he unpacked the groceries. "Oh well, it's just dinner," he thought, not realizing he had used the same excuse when he and Sara had first gone for coffee. Wine, of course. He hoped the checker didn't drink. Wine would clearly not be a good idea.

Chapter 7

Sara took Michael's clothes from the closet and put them in a pile by the front door. She assumed he would need them, and wanted it to be easy for him to get them and leave. Talking to him, seeing him without being able to touch, seemed unbearable. She was furious with herself for starting to cry as she collected them, angrily wiping the tears away as she carried first his shirts, then his sweaters, and then the pants he had hung in her large, walk-in closet to the entryway. The pants fit into the guest coat closet in the front.

Should she call and suggest a time for him to pick up the clothes, leaving a message on his answering machine when she knew he would be at work? She sighed – God, she was sighing all the time – and grabbed her cell, leaving a quick message for him. Even hearing his voice felt dreadful.

Nancy Alvarez

She wished she didn't have to look at his furniture, the few pieces he had brought to the condo because they complimented hers or had particular meaning for him. He was still there, but he wasn't, not in any meaningful way.

All of her friends were angry that he hadn't given her time to absorb his proposal, though Marty, who had been the most wary about her affair with the man in the first place, thought she should call or go over to his place and tell him she wanted to book the place she had found for the wedding, and was sorry she had been so silly.

The other women didn't think she was being silly; they thought he was acting just like a man: he had asked, which had clearly been difficult; she should have understood, and jumped in with both feet – forget her own doubts, or making peace with her memory of Jeffrey and the years they had spent together. All of them thought a group dinner in order, Elaine coming to pick up Sara, who was prevaricating, even though they had made a reservation at Volare, her favorite Italian restaurant in the Village.

The dinner was a success. About halfway through their appetizers, Sara realized she hadn't sighed since she had left her condo with Elaine. A miracle. The 'Vongole Al Fornno', a dish she and her friend Marty adored, was mouth watering as usual. Lucy reached over to spear a clam with her fork, which made all of them laugh. Someone then grabbed a bite of her calamari, and so it went. Even Sara laughed. Everyone noticed though no one said anything.

Then Marty, blunt as ever – she called it being direct which it was – said, "I don't know that I'd ever marry again. My marriage wasn't like yours and Jeffrey's, so I wouldn't feel the way you do about dishonoring Jonah, but still, what's the point?"

Elaine concurred. "That's true. We're certainly not going to have kids at our age, so why not just live together?" she asked.

"To make a statement about commitment and that this isn't just an arrangement," Sara found herself explaining. "Wow, I should have understood."

"Do you feel like you need to make a statement?" Lucy asked her.

"No…. But I mean, isn't moving in together a big statement? Why would we need more at this time of our lives?" she asked them as well as herself.

"That may be the way you feel, but clearly Michael wants the statement," Lucy gently suggested.

"Can we talk about something else?" Sara then asked. "You've all given me food for thought, but I need to stop agonizing about all this."

The conversation veered to Trump, which was certainly not a cheery subject, and then to the Mayor's race in New York. The entire group had supported de Blasio's second term, and was glad he had been re-elected. Elaine wanted to talk about her daughter's boyfriend, whom she adored but felt was impractical about life. Sara reminded her that he was only twenty-four. He had plenty of time to become more practical about his life choices. After all he had graduated from Brown, and would be able to earn a decent living at whatever career he decided to pursue.

Lucy laughed. "Just because you chose your life path in high school, doesn't mean most people do!"

"Right. Not everyone is submitting fashion drawings to Vogue at seventeen," Elaine agreed. She had been a very successful artist in the fashion world by the time she was a junior in college.

The conversation veered to children, again making Sara sad; why had she and Jeffrey postponed and then never gotten around to changing that decision. Of course if they had had children, then she would have had to deal with their feelings about Michael, her choice to live with him and then, if she could get past her own mixed feelings about marrying him, with their feelings about that.

Walking home she again felt grateful for her closest women friends, many of whom had been around since her college years; all had known Jeffrey and all had cheered her budding relationship with the handsome librarian. 'Perfect' for her, they had agreed. Sara had always been a bookworm, even in elementary school, and certainly in college and grad school.

She would have to give some thought to Elaine's idea about making a statement. But who was the statement for? Michael? And whom did he think it was for? The world, she supposed, his mother, and his friends as much as for themselves. Maybe understanding and feeling compassion for his need for a declaration would push her over the edge. She could bring him the chocolate pastries he loved with an apology and news about what else she had discovered about the place they had both liked the most for their service.

Maybe tomorrow, she thought, veering into the video store. Sometimes Netflix didn't have the newest films and a new film was exactly what her mood called for.

She only wondered what Michael was doing when she was ensconced on her couch. When they watched a video he always rubbed her feet.

. . . .

As Michael was walking home from the market, he realized he didn't even remember the checker's name. He wondered if he had ever known what it was; after all, who ever learned the names of the checkers at the supermarket? He unpacked his groceries

Tingle

quickly, showered, putting on his favorite cologne – the one Sara loved, he realized with a start – and then sat down to watch All In With Chris Hayes. He couldn't have concentrated enough to read the latest novel by Chimamanda Ngozi Adichie, one of his favorite novelists. She was a beautiful writer, smooth and thoughtful, and he always looked forward to her newest creation. By 6:30 he was chafing at the bit.

He tried not to think about why he was doing what he was doing. Hell, it was Sara who wasn't sure about marriage. It was Sara who needed time to 'think about it'. They hadn't talked about either of them dating during that time, and he certainly wasn't going to call and ask her permission he thought with some irritation. He had to wait outside the market for fifteen minutes before the checker came outside, enough time for guilt to rear its ugly head. When the young woman saw him, her face broke into a smile, which helped.

"I thought you might not show up," she said.

"Well, here I am," he declared. "All the way home I tried to remember your name, but I have to admit that I failed miserably."

Laughing, she told him, "Doreen."

"Mine's Michael," he said.

"I know," she admitted.

That surprised him. "How in the world did you learn my name?"

"I looked at one of your credit card receipts months ago," she said quietly, looking down. "Now isn't that embarrassing…."

"I think it's a kick," he replied, grabbing her hand and swinging it as they walked.

"We could eat out, or I could cook up something quickly at your place," she suggested, eyes twinkling. "Given all the stuff you bought today."

Even with his years of dating experience, the newfound brazenness of women still startled him. She was watching his face, noted the discomfort and laughed aloud.

"Yeah, I know. Dinner is just dinner, and I did buy a lot of food," he agreed. Then he turned to head back the way they had come.

They were both laughing when he opened his front door, though he couldn't have said about what. She was easy to talk to, and she had become more attractive with every step they had taken because she was both funny and smart. He wasn't surprised when she said she was going to night school, majoring in history. If she could make it through the masters program she wanted to teach African Studies. It might even be time to leave New York City if she landed a job someplace else.

While she was cutting vegetables for a casserole, he stood behind her and put his arms around her waist. "Are you sure you want to eat," she asked without turning.

"I'm not thinking of eating vegetables right now," he murmured into her tight little Afro.

"Oh…. I don't know what to say," she whispered.

"You don't have to say anything," he whispered in response.

Then she turned into his arms and he kissed her. It was only a short walk into his bedroom, and she didn't object. This time he didn't wonder what he was doing because that would have been too hypocritical, although Sara flew in and out of his mind like the flutter of butterfly wings. By the time she had disappeared he had pulled Doreen's skimpy silk sleeveless blouse over her head. Her half bra did little to cover her breasts, which were fuller than he expected. When he bent to kiss her nipples through the fabric, which he realized was part of his modus operandi, she moaned much as Sara did every time he bent to the same task. He quickly pushed aside that thought.

Tingle

Though he was fully erect by the time all of their clothes had fallen to the floor, he was aware that something didn't feel right. It wasn't even that he was being disloyal, or cheating – after all, they were taking a break, weren't they? – but that this woman didn't feel, smell or taste like Sara. He wanted Sara.

None of this made him stop what he was doing, and soon his head was between her legs, and he was parting her lips to more easily reach her clitoris. She came within seconds, which only heightened his arousal. He continued to flick his tongue over the hard little bump, and after a minor objection – "You don't have to do that again…" – Doreen said not another word. It took her longer to come the second time, but come she did, with a sustained moan and little grunts repeated over and over. He almost laughed, but instead entered her quickly. When he didn't come, she asked him if anything was wrong, which he denied. 'You aren't her' he thought, but then he came, more with a whimper than a bang. He hadn't known that coming could feel so different.

He realized there was no point in bedding another woman again during his month apart from Sara. Not only wasn't it satisfying, it was depressing. He lay there for several minutes, aware that leaving his bed would feel insulting to the woman beside him. Finally he slid his feet over the side.

Before he could stand up, she said, "There's someone else, isn't there?"

Why did women have to be so damned intuitive. His pause was enough.

"Then why?" she asked.

"I'm sorry," said Michael. "We agreed to take a break while she thought about my proposal…"

The woman beside him interrupted, "You asked her to marry you and you're here with me?"

"A mistake, I know," he admitted.

"No shit!" she said as she rose and grabbed her clothes from the floor. "We won't mention this the next time you come to the market," she warned and then, hopping to the door as she tried to put on her undies, she left the room. It only took seconds for him to hear his front door close, not even with a slam. Michael wondered how she had managed to put on her blouse and jeans so quickly.

He lay there feeling like a complete fool. A cad to both women, the one he loved and the one he had fantasized about for several years.

This little event was not one he would share with Sara, ever. How would she be able to forgive him? How would he forgive himself?

. . . .

Sara awoke with a start in the middle of the night, realizing she was sitting up before she even opened her eyes. She had no idea why she had awakened, but figured she had been dreaming, a nightmare, she supposed. She wondered if it had been about Michael, and then rolled out of the bed they had been sharing and made her way into the master bath for a glass of water, returning to bed as quickly as she could. She fell asleep almost immediately. When she awakened at her usual hour and turned on Amy Goodman, she didn't even remember waking during the night, let alone the dream that had made her actually sit up in bed.

When her phone rang she didn't answer because she was afraid it was Michael. She wasn't ready to speak to him, but felt guilty because she was sure he was calling about picking up his clothes. Later she played the message; she had been right. He said that he would stop by for his clothes at around 4:30 after he got off work. If that wasn't a convenient time, she could leave him a message to reschedule. It was as good a time as any, so she didn't return his call. She ran errands in the morning, thought of meeting one of her friends for lunch, but decided she didn't really want to talk to anybody about how it had felt to gather up all his clothes, let alone having to face him when he picked them up. She hoped he'd bring a big enough duffle.

Michael made it through the day, barely, and stopped at the market to apologize to Doreen before walking over to the condo. He thought of stopping again for a cup of coffee to fortify himself, but decided against. He knew Sara would be waiting.

She was waiting, at first sitting on her favorite reading chair with her feet up on the ottoman, but sitting was unbearable, so she had gotten up and begun to pace. At 4:25 she stopped pacing because she was afraid he would hear her and realize how nervous she was. She sat back down but didn't put her feet up. She forced herself to wait a few seconds after he rang the bell, and then stood, meandering over to the door though her stomach was roiling. She hoped she looked calm as she opened it.

He looked gorgeous. His handsome face broke into a smile when he saw her, and she realized she was returning it before she could give it any thought. Sara stepped aside so he could come inside. His clothes were behind her, on the wall next to the table in the entry hall she used for her purse, keys and other sundries. Instead of stooping to get the clothes, Michael took her in his arms and kissed her, the same open-mouthed kiss that always sent a tingle up her spine. Today was no exception. He tasted delicious, a mix of garlic, lemon, and Chile Verde. He had gone to their favorite little hole in the wall for lunch.

"Oh Michael," she groaned, ashamed of herself for melting so easily.

"God Sara," he sighed. "I have really missed you."

"Oh yes," she agreed. "This is horrible."

She didn't resist when he took her hand and led her along the hall to the bedroom they had been sharing for months. Before they could even reach the room, they were kissing with their usual passion, if anything intensified by their separation, and tearing at each other's clothes. There was nothing polite about their actions.

Michael pushed her onto the bed, unzipping her jeans with difficulty because his hands were shaking, and then he was pulling them over her hips, which she raised to make it easier, and down her legs. Then he was doing what he did best, at first through her panties, which were already wet anyway, and then they, too, were gone, slipped to her ankles. Again he kneeled between her thighs as she kicked them away, making a purring sound deep in her throat. It felt nothing to him like his foray with Doreen, and made it clear there was no one for him but Sara. Although he hadn't gone without sex for more than a few days since he had been sixteen, he would have to find a way. He'd have erections – after all he wasn't dead – but he didn't want to act on them, not with anyone else. He couldn't believe he could get this hard, and gritted his teeth.

"Oh, don't," she said, understanding immediately. She took his hard member into her mouth gently, not sucking, but licking and running her tongue up the length of the shaft, swirling it around the tip, concentrating on the ridge where it joined the rest. His hips rose because he couldn't control them, and then he was pushing her head away because he didn't want to come that way, and then he was inside her, both of them moving with urgency, faster and faster, until she cried out, Michael quickly following. He lay on top of her, unable to move. Then he realized he must be heavy and started to roll, but Sara held on to him so he couldn't.

Tingle

"Don't, not yet," she whispered. "Oh my God, how will we last a month?'

"I guess that's better than forever," he teased, being himself, being Michael.

"It wont be forever," she declared, surprised to see tears on his cheeks. She had no idea how to respond to his overt emotion. Finally she said, "I can't imagine life without you, Michael. That cannot happen."

"But…" he countered.

At first she was silent; then she, too, continued. "I need to accept the idea that I can marry again, and that it won't say something about my marriage to Jeffrey."

"I don't understand why marrying me would say anything about that," he replied as gently as he could.

"I don't either," she agreed. "At least in my head. It's my heart that's having trouble with it for some reason I don't really understand."

Michael's eyes were still full, but he managed to keep any tears from falling. He felt humiliated, and mumbled, "I hope you can figure it out soon."

"I will, I will, I know I will," she blurted, feeling awful about the pain she was causing him.

He reached for his clothes at the same time she reached for his arm. "Please wait for me, Michael."

"I'm trying," he mumbled as he slipped on his jockeys. He picked up his pants and walked out of the bedroom. He couldn't keep crying in front of her.

Sara wanted to jump out of bed and follow him, but realized she shouldn't do that. If she wanted 'room' she certainly had to give him the same. Hearing her front door close, gently this time, almost broke her heart.

What was wrong with her? Why was she causing pain to this man she so clearly loved, and to herself.

Lucy wasn't answering her cell, so she was probably in the pool swimming laps at her club. Sara decided to call Elaine, who wasn't as easy to talk to, because someone was better than no one.

She answered on the third ring. "Hi," came her cheerful voice. "I guess Lucy must be swimming."

Sara had to laugh. "Unfair but true." She paused. "Will you still talk to me?'

"Of course. What's up?" Elaine replied. "Wow, that was a loud sigh."

"I can't seem to stop doing that," Sara said.

"You do know how good Michael's been for you?" Elaine interrupted the next one.

Another sigh. "I know. So why can't I say 'yes'? Sara asked her.

"Jeffrey, I guess," Elaine replied.

"But you've all said he'd want me to be happy," Sara groaned.

"Exactly," her friend replied quietly.

"How do I do something I know I should, when I feel so damned uncomfortable about it?" Sara asked.

"I can give you the name of a good therapist," Elaine suggested.

"That would take too long. That's why I called you."

"What are the thoughts rolling around in that all-too-active head of yours?" Elaine asked, a very good question indeed.

Sara began by describing her wedding with Jeffrey, which she could still see in sharp relief. Her friend listened quietly, not interrupting. When Sara finished, paused, and then whispered, "I don't even feel guilty about all the sex we've had."

"And?" asked her friend.

Tingle

"If it's just an affair, it's somehow OK. If I marry him, then I'm really leaving Jeffrey," Sara mumbled, knowing how ridiculous that sounded but trying to explain anyway.

"He left you over a year ago, sweetie. Not purposely, but he left nonetheless," Elaine said.

Sara again started to cry. "I know this is silly, but I can't seem to help myself."

Elaine kept prodding. "OK, so tell me some of the other thoughts bumping around in there."

"I am the dirty little girl that neighbor called me when I was six or seven," she mumbled.

"You know what?" Elaine blurted. "Eric and I have been trying to update our oral sex experience, using you and Michael as a model."

Sara couldn't help but grin. "Doing what?" she asked.

Elaine grinned on the other end of the line too, though neither woman could see the other. "He's flicking his tongue really quickly over my clit, back and forth, back and forth, and wow, I'm coming so much easier!"

Sara shrugged. "Glad we're helping but I think anything new you try after 20 years would have the same effect."

"The point is," Elaine disagreed, "what we're trying is what you told me Michael does, and it's working. Eric and I are both thrilled," she gushed. "So you see, your adventures are helping us! Maybe we should call Marty and have her come over. I bet her sex life with Jonah has improved too."

"That's not fair," argued Sara. "It was never very good, even in the beginning."

Elaine wouldn't give up. "Yeah, but wouldn't it be fabulous if suddenly they were exploring and Marty was really enjoying it!"

"OK, you win. But that still doesn't mean I should marry Michael," she argued.

"Give me more," demanded Elaine.

"He's younger than I am," said Sara.

"By how many years?" Elaine asked.

"I'm not sure. A few."

"That's a good reason," Elaine said, the sarcasm dripping from her tongue.

"Ridiculous, I know," Sara agreed. "But I still can't seem to get myself to say 'yes'."

"I'm calling Marty. We'll be at your condo in under thirty."

They arrived twenty-five minutes later. Elaine had been filling the other woman in. Marty was appalled that Sara was so hesitant. "I think it's always a good idea to be careful, but I sure can't think of anything that's a red flag here," she declared.

"Wouldn't you wait if something happened to Eric or Jonah?" she asked her friends.

Almost in unison they both declared, "You've already waited a year!"

By the time the women left her condo, Sara had reached the conclusion she should marry Michael, but she still couldn't tell him that, she had said. She just couldn't.

Both of her friends had given up, and seemed pretty irritated with her. She was irritated with herself. Then she had the ludicrous thought: if Jeffrey was here he'd tell me what to do.

She grabbed a jacket since it was a bit chilly out, with fall on the way, and walked to Joe's Pizza on Carmine, a favorite of both hers and Jeffrey's. The guy behind the counter – was his name Joe? – said, "Hi Sara. The usual?" She nodded and he began to toss the dough. Sara couldn't even remember what 'the usual' was. When she opened the box at home, half the pizza was plain, the other covered in crumbled sausage and black olives. Her mouth watered from the scent and the flavors she could imagine just from looking at the pie.

When she bit into a slice of plain, the tears came again, unbidden. Jeffrey had always started with the sausage side, she with the plain. Now she would have to eat his pieces as well as her own. Even mixed with the salt of her tears, the pizza tasted delicious. She hadn't realized how hungry she was. Both Elaine and Marty had eaten Pepperidge Farm cookies with their coffee, but Sara had refrained. After all, she didn't want to get fat. That must have meant she wasn't going to stop seeing Michael, even if she couldn't get herself to say 'yes' to his proposal.

If he would continue to see her without her responding favorably to that idea right away.

Chapter 8

Michael realized he was feeling very angry again. He had never even asked a woman to live with him, and here he was, proposing marriage, and this woman wasn't sure she could marry him. He poured himself a shot of Glen Fiddich and sat down on his most comfortable living room chair. He rarely drank on weekdays, and certainly not before 5 o'clock, but today seemed a good time to break that habit. After a few sips, he felt calmer.

It wasn't Sara's fault that he had never wanted to live with a woman before. And it wasn't her fault that she needed time to think about marrying for a second time. Her reaction was actually pretty normal. Except for the part about dishonoring Jeffrey, her husband of many years, by marrying again. That was kind of nuts.

Did he ever act in ways that were nuts? Maybe never daring to live with a woman had been crazy, though he had certainly never looked at it that way. Of course most people didn't see their outlandish behavior as nuts: it was just the way they were.

Maybe he had proposed because he was overcome by his feelings for Sara, and the fact that he had never felt this way before. He had never wanted to live with any of his women, even the few he had 'dated' for more than a year. He loved living with Sara in her condo, and it wasn't because it was a great space, lovely in design and decoration, not fancy but comfortable and certainly esthetically pleasing. He loved coming home from a long day at the library to the sound of Sara humming in her kitchen, preparing their dinner. He loved crawling into bed with her every night. He loved their conversations, wide-ranging and deep. He loved her take on most matters, her prescient incites into things as diverse as the latest political disasters in the country to the troubles of her closest friends.

He loved her very being.

How could she not want to marry him?

'Calm down' he reminded himself. She hasn't said she doesn't want to marry you; she has been very clear that she has to take in the idea, figure it out, and decide if she wants to marry for a second time. That has nothing to do with the way she feels about you.

'Doesn't it?'

Odd, but the person he was thinking about calling to talk about his feelings was Sara's best friend, Lucy. Before he could change his mind, he picked up his cell and dialed her number.

"Hello Lucy. It's Michael," he said. When she didn't respond immediately, he added, "Sara's partner."

"I know that, Michael. I was just startled to hear your voice. Sorry I didn't say 'hi' right away. I'd ask you why you're calling, but I know why," she said.

"I don't know why I'm not calling one of my own friends," he began but Lucy interrupted with a laugh.

"In my experience," she finally managed. "Men rarely talk to each other about their feelings."

"So I've been told," he sighed, and then added, "Now I'm imitating her."

"Michael, I don't think I understand why she's hesitating any more than you do, but if I've learned anything over the years, it's to trust Sara's process," she said.

"And if she says she can't?" he asked.

"I guess you'll have to decide if you can live with her, even forever, without getting married," came her reply, hesitant but clear. Then she added, "You just can't break up!"

"Why not?" he asked, surprised.

"Because it's obvious to all of us how much you love each other," she replied.

"She's not just bonking the hot library stud?" he asked with a chuckle, though he didn't understand how he could find anything humorous in the situation.

"At first that's what we all thought it was about, passion, for both of you. But it became obvious pretty quickly that what you guys were sharing was much more than that," she answered, immediately asking, "How would you feel if you broke up with her over this?"

"Horrible," he groaned.

"Well, that's something to pay attention to," she suggested.

"Yes, it is. I can see why Sara has relied on you for so long," he said.

"We've relied upon each other. I can't be as honest with anyone else, and that's been true for years," she explained.

"That's also something to pay attention to. I feel the same way," he had to admit.

"Oh Michael. Give her the month if you can bear it. We're talking daily, and I do think she should accept your proposal. I know figuring out why it feels like abandoning Jeffrey will help her," she added.

"Are we very different?" Michael asked with some hesitation, although he wasn't sure he really wanted to know.

Surprised, Lucy replied, "I hadn't thought about that. But you know, in some ways you're similar."

"How?" he immediately asked.

"You're both very sensitive, and both talk about feelings more than most men. And that's a bigee. I think Jeffrey was more of a dreamer," she added, pausing.

"I was forced to be practical from a very early age," he muttered.

"I'm sure you were, and that makes sense. If you could have dreamed a different life, a different path, do you have any idea what it might have been?" she asked him.

"What a great question," he replied. "Maybe I would have become a social worker, working with kids. Huh, I never gave that much thought – it would have taken too many years of schooling, I guess."

He could hear the shrug in her voice. "You could volunteer."

"If she turns me down and decides she has to stop seeing me, I'll certainly have enough time on my hands," he mused, his laugh lacking in humor.

"Michael," Lucy sternly admonished him. "She is not breaking up with you and has no intention of doing so, or she would never have asked you to move into her condo."

"Shit. I hate this," he said.

"She does too, if that makes you feel any better," Lucy told him.

Tingle

"Not much. I miss the hell out of her," he admitted.

"Maybe you could both figure this out while you're living together," Lucy wondered aloud. When he was silent, she added, "Though taking this break won't kill either one of you."

"I don't know if I didn't let myself love anybody before, or if I chose women I knew I wouldn't feel that way about, because when there are problems it hurts too damned much if there's love too," he wondered.

"That seems like a waste to me, but understandable. Thank God for Jason! I think that a lot," Lucy said.

"You seem to be a very good match," he said.

"When we're not fighting," Lucy laughed in response.

"Do you do a lot of that," he asked, genuinely curious.

She replied, "Not much anymore. But the first few years, we had quite a few drag outs. Funny, but I don't remember what any of them were about," she mused.

"We haven't fought about anything much, until this," Michael said. "God, maybe I shouldn't have asked her, or I should have brought it up gradually. Or waited 'til we'd been living together longer."

"Don't second guess yourself. No point," Lucy said.

"Thanks, Luce. You've given me lots to think about. Maybe I'll call her tomorrow and say I've thought about it some more and think we should figure this out while we're living together," he said.

"I think that's actually a very good idea," Sara's friend agreed. "I can suggest that to Sara too. We're having tea tomorrow afternoon."

"OK. I'll wait a few more days so she has time to think about it before I make the same suggestion," he said.

When he hung up he realized he was no longer angry, but he still finished the Glen Fiddich.

. . . .

Totally shocked by Lucy's suggestion, Sara bleated, "You think I should let him move back in while we deal with the marriage issue?"

"How can it hurt?" Lucy asked in return.

Sara was tired of sighing. "He could talk me into it," she lamely muttered.

"Oh please!" replied her best friend.

"I don't feel strong around him," Sara tried to explain.

"Then buck up!" Lucy ordered.

"Jeez. You're supposed to be on my side," Sara whined.

"Did it ever dawn on you that I am?" Lucy asked her, sounding irritated.

"You like him," Sara said, as if she was surprised.

"I love him, you idiot, and so do you," Lucy replied.

Another sigh. "Yeah, but does that mean I have to marry him?"

"No, honey, it doesn't. But I think if you two live together, you might figure that out together, rather than agonizing by yourselves."

That upset Sara, who whispered, "I didn't know he was agonizing."

"Sara, you are being a ninny," said Lucy.

"Gee thanks," mumbled Sara. "You really think he should move back in?"

This time Lucy sighed before replying, "Yes!"

Then she suggested, "Just think about it, but don't take too long. Now, enough about that. How's your writing going?"

"I haven't been writing," Sara acknowledged.

"Maybe you should get back to it. Writing could help clear your mind, to say nothing of your heart," Lucy suggested. "Let's eat. I'm starving."

Sara didn't think she was hungry, but ate her entire triple-decker BLT and then had a piece of cherry pie. Afterwards she felt much better.

Tingle

Michael called about an hour after she got home. He had not been able to wait. Her heart pounded in her chest as soon as she heard his voice.

"Hey Sara. I've been thinking about all this, and I need to apologize for just dumping my proposal on you," he began.

"You didn't dump anything. We were having a special day and it was just a natural outcome of our trip," Sara disagreed.

"I still don't want you to feel pressured by one good day, but I do have a suggestion," he continued.

"And what's that?" she asked, curious.

"I think I was wrong to suggest we figure this out separately, living apart," he continued, though he had trouble getting the words out. He was not used to admitting he was wrong, and here he was doing it twice in five minutes.

"You and Lucy are in cahoots," Sara muttered.

"What are you talking about?" he asked, though of course he knew.

Sara sighed. "I am getting really sick of sighing."

"Then don't. I could bring my things back there after work. I haven't even unpacked anything. So what do you say?" he asked, heart pounding.

"Mr. Neat has his stuff in a duffel?" she teased.

"Very funny. And you're prevaricating," he replied.

"What do you want for dinner?" Sara asked. Michael wanted to jump in the air and raise his fist in the Olympic salute, but instead merely thanked her for the invite.

"Anything you want to make is fine by me," was his reply.

"Yeah, but what's your favorite?" she kept at it.

The woman was something else. "I really love your yoghurt chicken," he said.

She nodded to herself, and declared, "You got it."

After work he walked back to his old apartment, his tenant relieved that he was picking up his clothes and the few other items he had brought back there from Sara's just a few days before. "Good choice," she told her landlord.

"What do you know?" Michael laughed.

"More than you do," came her reply.

Michael picked up the black duffel, his clothes still folded neatly inside, and carried it over to Sara's slung over his back. He grinned all the way there. Sara was grinning too when she opened her front door. She had heard him in the hall and had known he would have trouble getting out his keys if he had brought back all of his stuff.

"Let's eat first," she said.

"I'm ravenous, so that sounds good," Michael agreed.

They tucked in to the chicken, which they both poured over the rice on their plates. Michael loaded up with green beans and salad as well, his plate overflowing, which did Sara's heart good. She waited to eat her greens until she had finished the chicken and rice.

"What's for dessert," Michael asked as he pushed away from the table. Undoing the top button of his chinos he groaned, "Thank God, some room!"

"What do you think?" she asked him. She had made cherry cheesecake, his favorite. "I think if I cut you a piece you're going to have to do more than unbutton the top button."

He stood and shucked his pants, sitting back down in his jockeys. His erection stood out from the flap of his fly front.

"What do you want first?" she asked with a huge smile.

He grabbed her hand across the table, rose and pulled her into the bedroom. She dropped to her knees when they reached the bed.

Tingle

"Not on you life," he growled. "My turn." He sat her on the bed, rolling down her lace undies after having pulled aside the crotch to give her a little taste of what was to come.

"Oh come on, not fair," she moaned.

His tongue was busy so he couldn't really respond, though his actions were certainly a response of sorts. After she came his fingers danced along her labia until she cried out and came a second time. When he again bent over her, she begged him to stop.

"Are you sure?" he asked, grinning broadly and licking his lips.

She grabbed his hips, urging him down. "Come on. Come on. I need you inside me."

"My favorite place," he whispered as he followed her command. Sara began to move her hips before he could, first quickly, and then slowing down to extend his pleasure.

"Jesus!" he gasped. "You're evil, lady."

"So I was told as a child," she panted. "God, I'm going to come again."

"That's the idea," he said, and then exploded inside her. She came seconds after he did, both of them collapsing on the bed. He lay half on top of her and half on the mattress because Sara wouldn't let him roll off completely.

"I feel marvelous," she sighed.

"So do I," he sighed as well.

They lay there wrapped around each other, limp and content.

It was Sara who broke the silence. "Chocolate. I want chocolate."

"What about the cheesecake?" he reminded her.

"You can have that. I have a dark chocolate bar with cherries and almonds in my pantry," she said, slowly rising and moving, naked, back into the kitchen. She stood at the counter totally comfortable with her nakedness, cutting him a huge piece of the cheesecake.

"That's too big," he complained, but she just shrugged. "Wanna bet?"

Not only did he finish that piece, standing naked beside her, but he cut himself a second, albeit smaller piece, before sitting at the small round kitchen table.

And thus they fell back into their old routine, sometimes making love before they ate dinner, sometimes eating, relaxing on her couch and then repairing to their bedroom.

Energized, Sara had no trouble returning to her novel, outlining the entire 12 chapters easily. By the time Michael had again been living in the condo for almost a month, she was ready to begin the actual writing. Instead of finding the idea daunting, she couldn't wait to begin.

Michael was good for her.

He enjoyed his hours at the library as he had before, suggesting reading material for his favorite library patrons and encouraging new visitors with his affable smile and obvious breadth of knowledge.

He still knew that it was very important to him that Sara say 'yes' to his proposal. It wasn't that he had changed his views on commitment or marriage, but that he wanted to marry her. He had allowed an intimacy to develop that was new to him and marvelous, and he wanted them both to honor what they had with a license and ceremony.

She hadn't said anything to him about whether she was still doing research on the places in New Jersey and he was afraid to ask. He had decided just a few days before he had moved back into her condo – 'theirs', she kept reminding him, though that didn't feel accurate to him – that he wouldn't ask or push her about the proposal or the 'where or when' of it. Better to let their intimacy grow and become stronger. Then he would raise the issue again. He could also try to figure out why it mattered to him so much, and then find a way to explain it to her.

As for Sara, she didn't mention marriage because she was still mulling over everything she was trying to figure out, hoping her monthly lunch with her friends would help her. At their next meeting they spent the first half hour sipping wine and talking about marriage, Sara's doubts, and how to resolve them. None of the women believed in prevarication.

"You haven't even had the little problems all the rest of us have experienced and made peace with, and you're hesitating?" Elaine had exclaimed at one point.

Lucy had not agreed. "Some of the little stuff Jason and I have had to accept took months. And some of our issues didn't rear their heads until we'd been married for years, so I don't think that's fair."

"What kinds of 'little' stuff," Sara asked them both. She knew she would have to try to remember the issues that had been trouble spots for her and Jeffrey. It all seemed so long ago.

Her friends made a list by going around the table.

> Who makes the meals, and when;
>
> Who does cleanup;
>
> Who does the grocery shopping and even on which day or week;
>
> Who takes the laundry to the basement and
>
> Who picks it up;
>
> Who folds the clothes;
>
> When they should talk about serious stuff;
>
> When they just 'talk' because they like to;
>
> How they spend their 'together' time;

How they decide who prevails when they disagree;
How they resolve actual fights.

And that was just the beginning of the list.

None of the individual issues seemed all that important, but taken as a whole when two completely different individuals join lives, even silly differences can seem, or even become, looming.

Sara had to admit that she and Michael appeared to have resolved most of those things naturally, and hadn't even had to talk about them. Lucy suggested she sit down with him and bring the subject up. Bringing those kinds of differences out in the open, and agreeing upon solutions for them as much as possible, might preclude larger problems developing as the relationship continued.

"Married or not," Marty added.

At their age, the friends all agreed, having a ring wouldn't make a difference in solving those 'little' problems.

"That's just it," Sara said quietly. "Then why marry? We're not going to have kids at this point in our lives."

"To make a statement I guess," Lucy replied with a shrug.

"That's what Michael's been saying, but he also said he'd give more thought to why taking that plunge feels so important to him," Sara agreed.

"You could go to that resort place you found in the Pine Barrens and have a little ceremony by yourselves where you 'pledge your troth', so to speak," Marty suggested. "That would make a statement, don't you all think?"

Lucy wasn't sure that would be enough for Michael.

Elaine looked perturbed. "Involving the government in our personal lives, especially at this point in American history, seems like something to avoid if you can," she mused.

Even Lucy had to agree. "You could draw up a prenup, and check with a lawyer I know to make sure it says all that it needs to."

"I know that if I predeceased Michael I would leave my condo to him, because neither of us has kids," Sara said.

Everyone agreed that was a good idea, sensible and fair.

"Why would I want to draw up a 'prenup' if we're not going to get married?" Sara asked in almost a whisper.

Lucy responded. "I guess because it's a kind of statement of commitment, even if you can't get past the idea that you're abandoning Jeffrey."

"My feelings are hurting Michael, and he doesn't deserve it," Sara said.

"Feelings are feelings, as my former therapist used to tell me. They're not good or bad, they're just feelings. I don't think they can be ridiculous," Lucy said as she reached across the table to squeeze her hand.

Elaine disagreed. "I don't think it's your feelings that are hurting him anyway, but the fact that he's finally asked a woman to marry him, has wanted to take that step, and you're not sure you can."

Marty chimed in. "I think that hits the nail on the proverbial head."

Sara continued to think aloud. "I love him. And I never thought I'd feel love for a man again. He's a great person. He's funny and smart and caring. I'm really fortunate, I know I am, so why is this so difficult?"

"You were married to Jeffrey for over twenty years. A year and a few months isn't a very long time to adjust to changing your life completely and starting over," Marty said.

"But if I ask him to give me a little more time, and I can't get past this, isn't that unfair," she asked her friends.

"He knows you're confused and struggling. It's not like it's something you're hiding," Elaine reminded her.

On the way home, a brilliant idea popped into Sara's head. She could go to the Jersey shore, where she and Jeffrey were married, walk along the beach he loved, and try to talk to him about it. Lucy wouldn't think this was a crazy idea, though Marty probably would. At least she'd think it was a bit woo-woo. It was, but it also made Sara feel tremendous relief.

She didn't tell anyone what she was thinking of doing, not Lucy or Michael, who might or might not have understood. She knew she had to try it, even if the two people she loved most in the world didn't understand. And she didn't want anyone to dissuade her.

She spent the next couple of days taking care of business, paying bills, and preparing an extra meal so she could drive to Jersey and not have to hurry back to cook. She wanted to have a full day in Deal with nothing to take care of when she got home.

A few minutes after Michael left for work on Thursday she walked over to the garage where she parked her car, and was driving through the Holland Tunnel by 9:30. She felt lighter than she had in weeks.

When she reached Deal, she was quite surprised by how much the place had changed. The big homes were the same, but there were apartment buildings as well, and shops, and bike paths – bike paths! – Jeffrey would have loved that. The landscape looked so different she wasn't sure where they had walked all those years ago. The little temple where they had been married was nowhere to be seen. She had hoped to use that as a starting point to find her way, but parked, deciding that just being on the beach would have to suffice.

She stood on the bike path and untied her tennis shoes, stuffing her socks in the pockets of her zippered sweatshirt. As soon as she

Tingle

felt the soft, warm white sand under her feet, she knew she had made the perfect choice. She curled her toes into the sand, a ritual she and Jeffrey had indulged in every time they visited the shore, though in recent years they had rented a place in Ocean Beach on Fire Island.

It was a little eerie but she could almost feel his hand around her waist.

"Kiddo, you've got to move on, have a life," she heard him say, his deep basso as soothing as it had always been, even if was just reverberating in her head.

Sara ducked her head so no one could see her cry, even though there wasn't anyone else on the beach. It wasn't July or August, and it was a workday.

She knew that was exactly what he would say to her: 'Sweetheart, you have to move on.' She had to let herself love again and commit to that love, just as she had committed to him.

She wasn't sure if it made it easier or harder that he would have liked Michael. "Way to go!" he might have said, though he probably would have been a little jealous that the guy was so damned good looking.

Chapter 9

After walking on the Deal beach, it became easier for Sara to accept that she not only loved Michael, but was going to marry him. It almost felt as if Jeffrey was supporting her, which she realized was ridiculous no matter what Lucy said about feelings being just feelings. She knew she wouldn't even tell her about Deal, although Lucy probably would have laughed aloud as she gave her a big hug. Sara had no idea how she was going to explain her experience to Michael, who she feared would just find Jeffrey's 'approval' insulting. She knew she had to try. Keeping something so important secret would damage what they were building, possibly irreparably. She slid into her car feeling much lighter than she had driving to Jersey from the City.

. . . .

Michael was miserable. Because of his workload, and the intensity of his relationship with Sara, he rarely saw any of the few friends he considered close ones. With a start he realized he hadn't even spoken to Jevon, the only man with whom he shared some of his feelings. There weren't many over the years, but some. All this time he had told himself that was just what men did, or didn't do as it were. He was startled to realize he didn't know much about Jevon's relationship with Margery, whom he'd been living with for at least a year, not more than the basics, and that his friend seemed truly happy. Nevertheless Jevon was the one person he thought he could talk to now. On his first break he looked up his number in the little address book he always carried with him but rarely used, and dialed. He told himself he'd add the number to his contact list in his cell phone; he really was old-fashioned, which Sara frequently teased him about. Jevon, who was an editor for a small publishing company, often worked at home, and much to Michael's relief, this day was no exception. Jevon did sound surprised to hear from him during a work day, but immediately suggested Michael come by if he could get someone to cover for him at the library.

"You sound pretty stressed out for someone's who's known for being cool and collected, my friend," he said.

Michael didn't know he was seen that way, but immediately told Jevon he thought the part time girl would cover for him, which she was more than willing to do, laughing, "But you'll owe me," as he grabbed his shoulder bag and headed for the exit.

"'Cool and collected', he thought, 'huh….'

Jevon was waiting by his open door, a quizzical look on his face. He ushered Michael inside without a word. When they were sitting across from each other in his small living room and Michael hadn't said anything, Jevon prodded, "So?"

Michael's response was so soft-spoken, Jevon barely heard him.

Tingle

"I've been dating someone and it's become pretty serious," he murmured.

That did raise an eyebrow. "That's a surprise, my man," Jevon said. Though he didn't know details of his friend's love life, he knew that no woman remained in Michael's orbit for very long. He and Margery had even talked about it a couple of times, agreeing there was no point in saying anything to Michael. After all, it was his business.

"Sara has been coming to the library for years – her name's Sara …" he began, Jevon interrupting with a grin and "I figured," which almost made Michael smile.

Instead he took a deep breath and blurted, "She's white!"

"No shit!" Jevon exclaimed before he could stop himself. He was obviously shocked. None of their circle had ever dated a white woman, let alone become serious with one. "Wow. I don't know what to say."

"Me neither, but I'm going to try," Michael replied. "At first we just talked about books, ones I recommended and ones she had read on her own and suggested to me, and then we started meeting for coffee – well, it was supposed to be coffee – so we had longer to talk about them," he added.

"Coffee would have been safer," came his friend's wry response. "What did you actually imbibe?" he asked curiously.

"You know that little wine bar near the library?" Michael asked in return.

"Nice place," Jevon agreed. "I can see why you went there instead of Starbucks."

"And all we did was talk about books for weeks, but over time we became curious about each other, and started to ask personal questions."

He continued, "Her husband died about a year ago. They were married a long time," as if that would explain what eventually happened.

"So she was vulnerable," Jevon nodded, thinking he understood.

"No. I mean, yes, she was, but that wasn't why I pursued more. Or why she did. It just evolved, I guess. Before either of us was even aware of it, we were intimate, at least in the emotional sense." He paused, but Jevon was silent, waiting for him to resume.

"OK," Michael said defensively. "I don't know why I leaned down and kissed her one afternoon as we were saying 'good-bye' and I shouldn't have, I know, but it happened before I gave it any thought. It just felt completely natural," he finished, letting his final words hang in the air lamely. Embarrassed, he tried to explain further. "She kissed me back, though I don't think she expected to do that either."

"Tongues touching," came Jevon's first, and ironic, words.

"Oh for God's sake," Michael exclaimed, exasperated.

"Trying to lighten the mood. Sorry," Jevon apologized.

"It was electric. There's no other word for how it felt," Michael continued, despite feeling irritated.

"Did you go to your place right away?" Jevon asked him.

"No. I think we were both too shocked by what had happened," Michael replied.

"And," Jevon again prodded, finally curious.

"I don't remember what happened next. I think we talked again at the wine bar, and decided we would just be friends," he said, clearly trying to remember the sequence of events.

"How long were you able to 'just be friends'?" Jevon asked.

Again Michael sighed, saying, "That's what Sara does, she sighs. I don't know. I'm trying to remember."

"Wow, that hot huh?" Jevon teased.

Tingle

"Yeah, actually. I've never felt this way with anyone before," Michael muttered. Jevon was at a loss for words. With obvious surprise, Michael added, "I've been living with her for about a month."

His friend's mouth actually fell open, which made Michael smile. "I always thought that was just an expression…."

"What was?" Jevon asked him, confused.

"His mouth fell open."

"We really haven't seen each other in a long time. Wow! What'd you do with your apartment?" he asked Michael.

"A friend of a friend of hers is renting it while she looks for something permanent. She just moved here," Michael replied.

"I never thought you'd ever let someone into you life. How does it feel living with her," Jevon asked.

"Much to my surprise, it's been pretty easy," Michael admitted, holding up his hands. "Don't say it. I know it won't always be easy; there'll be problems, but…"

"But?"

"I trust we'll be able to work them out. I've never been able to talk to anyone the way I can with Sara. It's kind of amazing," he said.

"I'll say," Jevon agreed.

"Can you talk to Margery about what you feel?" Michael asked, surprised he had never thought to ask his friend anything like that over all the years of their friendship.

Jevon grinned, "More than I have with anyone else." He paused and then added, "A guy thing."

"It's sure what we've been taught. I just… I don't know. She asked a lot of questions," Michael explained, though he knew that didn't really explain much of anything.

"After awhile Margery gave up, though occasionally she still gets the question bug," Jevon said.

"You might try answering. I know you two are committed for life, but who knows, having someone who eventually knows almost everything might actually feel good," Michael suggested.

"We should all have dinner. But if we do that, and the two women become friends if they can get over the color thing, then I could be in real trouble," Jevon laughed.

"That would take time, given the color thing, so you have plenty of time to prepare," Michael teased. "This is really crazy, isn't it?"

The two friends sat across from each other, sipping their coffee, comfortable with the silence. In truth, the two were more comfortable with silence than with sharing.

"This is gonna be a shocker," Michael began.

"More than what you've already told me," Jevon blurted. "Come on!"

"I've asked her to marry me."

"No shit!"

"It gets worse. She's not sure she can," Michael added though he clearly didn't want to.

Jevon frowned. "Yeah, that color thing really gets in the way."

Michael demurred. "It isn't that. Really. And if I believe her, you can too. She says it feels like dishonoring what she had with Jeffrey, her husband."

"I can kind of understand that," Jevon said.

"You can?"

Jevon patted his arm. "If you've been married for a long time, and feel good about it, taking that plunge with someone else, well, I think it'd be really hard."

Tingle

"If Margery died, God forbid?" Michael asked him.

Jevon, being Jevon, turned the question into a joke. "I'd sure fool around…."

"I need you to take this seriously. I'm really upset and need you to listen. I don't know how to forgive her for not saying 'yes' right away. I mean I've never even considered living with anyone before her," Michael said.

"To tell the truth, I can't picture life without Margery. I really love the lady," Jevon responded. "Maybe I should try talking to her a little bit more about stuff."

"It sure feels different when you do. Maybe women are right and men are just idiots," Michael suggested.

"Yeah, but enough for today. This conversation is churning up my innards," Jevon said.

He stood to make sure Michael understood he had had enough, and grabbed his friend's jacket. At the door Michael turned back to ask him, "Do you think you and Margery would have dinner with us sometime soon?"

"You bet. She's gonna be dyin' to meet this woman, and I am too," Jevon nodded in agreement. "Come up with a few different times and I'll talk to Margery about it."

"You'll be polite…?" Michael asked quietly.

"Come on man, what do you take me for? And you know Margery will. It's part of her nature," the other man said as he held the door for Michael.

"Give her time, Michael. She really does sound special," he suggested.

Jevon leaned against the door after his friend had pulled it closed, totally blown away. 'This'll sure provoke some talking,' he thought as he walked into the kitchen. He had no idea if his almost-wife would be more pleased that their friend had finally found a woman he could love or upset that the woman was white. A drink was called for, he decided, the hell with working anymore. He poured himself a tumbler of Laphroaig. He had no idea how Michael was going to get through an entire afternoon of work. It wasn't even his problem, but he couldn't imagine sitting down at his desk.

Michael found himself wondering if he and Jevon would begin to talk more regularly about things that really meant something to them. He realized he would actually like it if they did. Sara had opened more worlds for him than he had known he even missed.

. . . .

When she walked into the library Michael was helping a library patron, as usual. When the man walked away from his reference desk and Michael looked up, he was startled to see Sara standing in front of him as if she was his next customer.

"Would you meet me at our wine bar," she asked with no preamble.

He merely nodded, the lump in his throat preventing a verbal response, which of course Sara didn't know. She just thought he still didn't want to talk to her but was being his typically kind self. Which was better than nothing.

She left the library with a half hour to spare. It was only 4 o'clock, so he wouldn't arrive at their meeting place for at least a half hour. He rarely left exactly at four, either taking the time to finish helping a customer, or to clean up his desk and then collect his things. She thought about going inside the wine bar herself and ordering a glass for fortification, but sitting still for that long seemed beyond her, so she began to walk. She headed for Washington Square – maybe there would be some stray musicians playing – but found it relatively empty for that time of day. She walked around the circumference, checking her watch frequently, surprised at how quickly she was able to traverse the familiar place. At this rate she'd have to circle the park three or even four times to arrive at the wine bar on time, or even a little bit early. After the second loop she decided another would be unbearably boring, and instead walked over to her favorite coffee shop on East Eighth Street and ordered a latte. She sat at a table by the window and sipped, watching the people walk by as a diversion. There were always interesting looking people strolling the Village streets. At 4:25 she could no longer sit still, quickly found a few bills in her purse for a tip, stood, and headed for the wine bar.

Michael was already there, looking sad. Before Sara sat down across from him, she leaned down and brushed his lips with her own. He almost pulled away, but didn't.

"I drove out to New Jersey yesterday," she said with no preamble. He raised his eyebrows, assuming she meant the Pine Barrens, which she understood immediately.

"No," she demurred. "I went to Deal."

When he didn't respond – he had no idea why she would have gone to Deal – Sara explained, "That's where Jeffrey and I were married."

"Ah," was all he could manage.

"I want to tell you about my experience, even though it won't be easy for either one of us."

Michael couldn't help but smile. "Could I stop you?" he asked.

"No," she replied, smiling too. He knew her well. When she set her mind to something there was no stopping her.

"At first I couldn't even find the beach we loved, because everything had changed," she began.

Michael wished she would cut to the chase. His heart was pounding: would this be the end?

"Anyway, I finally did. I walked for quite awhile." She paused, which made Michael's heart pound even harder. "This is going to sound weird, I know, but it kind of felt, after awhile, that I was talking to Jeffrey."

'Uh oh,' he thought.

"And he was kind of giving me permission," she gulped. "Weird, I know."

"Kind of, but go on," Michael urged. Maybe this wasn't the end.

"So, I feel like he did. I mean, even more than that," she continued. Another pause. "I could hear Lucy telling me Jeffrey would want me to love again, and that was what it felt like he was saying," she murmured. Her sigh was deep and heartfelt.

Michael wanted to shout, "Do you actually need his permission?" but refrained since it felt like this was going where he hadn't had the courage to believe it would.

"So, yes," Sara said, taking his hand. "I'll marry you," immediately adding, "Are you mad it kind of took my former husband's permission?"

"No. I'm just relieved you're saying 'yes'," he said.

"I think I finally said goodbye to him too," Sara added, squeezing Michael's hand.

Chapter 10

They lay on their backs, one of Michael's legs carelessly thrown over Sara's, utterly spent. They had walked, then run, to her condo, stripping clothes from each other's bodies as they tumbled in the front door and leapfrogged to the bedroom. It had felt as if they had made love for hours, though only an hour had passed. Michael sighed with contentment. Sara turned to look at him with a broad grin.

"Mmmmm," he murmured, grinning as well. "I think my tenant has found a temporary place, but nothing permanent. She'd have to give notice but I'm sure she'll come back very happily."

"Are you sure you want to give up the apartment?" Sara asked, clearly concerned about the idea.

At that he turned, startled. "Why wouldn't I?"

She sighed with relief. "I have no idea, but I had to let you decide."

Michael kissed one cheek and then the other. "If you want to help we can start packing the stuff I haven't brought over here when I get off tomorrow."

"I would love to!" she declared with such force they both laughed aloud. Then they both fell silent, each lost in their own thoughts.

"Maybe we should find someone to marry us and do it privately, and then have a party after we get back from our honeymoon," she dreamily suggested.

"And where are we doing that?" he asked her.

"I love water," she murmured.

"So do I. How about driving up to the Cape to check it out?" he suggested.

"How about going back to the Pine Barrens. The place has special meaning for us and I'm sure that Justice of the Peace we met in the coffee shop would say the right words and tell us where to get the proper papers."

"I don't know. In Provincetown there probably wouldn't be many raised eyebrows at a mixed marriage," he countered.

With surprise, Sara replied, "In this day and age I don't think that would be a problem anywhere."

At that, Michael raised a brow.

"OK," she said with a shrug. "I guess I have a lot to learn."

Michael squeezed her hand. "Yes, no doubt."

After Michael left for the library the next morning, Sara opened her laptop and began to search for 'places to marry' in both areas just to be thorough, and found a slew of them. Before starting to call, she switched to Bed & Breakfast listings, pleased to discover several in town or right on the beach near Provincetown as well as

Tingle

in the Pine Barrens. Most of them even had exterior and interior pictures to peruse. She put several in her dock to show Michael, very excited by the prospects she had found. Then she took a deep breath – was she really going to do this? – and picked up the phone. She loved this man, and she had loved being married to Jeffrey too, and yes, she was really doing this! She thought she might check in with Lucy, but decided she didn't have to and set the phone back on its stand. Marrying Michael was not just exciting, it was right.

By the time she was waiting outside the library to walk over to his apartment to begin packing boxes she was at peace. They grabbed at least five each from the Gristedes on the corner on their way there. They held hands – even though it meant juggling the cardboard boxes: it was worth it – swinging them back and forth as they walked, which elicited smiles from several passers-by. So much for New Yorkers being disturbed by ebony and ivory. Michael headed for his bedroom and Sara to the three bookcases in the living room, stuffed to the brim, and overflowing.

"I think you have more books than I do, which shouldn't be surprising given what you do," she called out.

"I've been thinking about where we could put them all," he called back. "I have a friend who's a carpenter and I could assist," he said, standing in the hallway by the living room.

She squinted, picturing her living room and the hallway to her office and their bedroom. "D'ya think the hallway would be wide enough to line one wall with bookcases?"

"Like minds," he grinned. "Bobby works with me. You haven't met him because he works in the back. I'll ask him to come over tomorrow night to measure, if you don't have other plans."

"Do," she agreed, vigorously shaking her head. "I could put up a stew in the crock pot tomorrow morning, so why don't you also invite him for supper," she added.

"His significant other is out of town, so I'm sure he'd love that. She does most of the cooking," he explained.

"Typical," she quipped, hands on hips.

"Won't be true here. I love to cook!" he declared though he didn't have to. Sara loved eating his concoctions as much as he loved making them.

She put down the box she was holding, walked over to him, put her arms around him, and snuggled in. "You know what one of the things I liked most about this, from the beginning? Stop cackling. Besides that," she giggled, feeling like her fifteen-year-old self.

Michael thought about it for only a few seconds, and exclaimed, "Cooking together!"

"You bet. And I expect us to continue doing that for..."

Before she could finish her sentence he added, "...ever!"

"I love that word, especially when you say it."

With his fingers already working the zipper on the back of her striped tan slacks, he pulled her towards the bedroom.

"Time for a break."

"But we haven't even been working for an hour," she objected without much force. After all, they had the whole evening, and the one after that and on and on. Sara loved the sound of that too.

Michael held on to Sara's hand, and she followed him meekly to the bedroom. His eyes sparkled, because he immediately understood the game. He sat her down on the bed, and knelt to take off her shoes, which he had to untie, and then rolled her socks down to the ankle and off each foot as if she was a child. He rose to his knees, which

Tingle

made Sara gasp, a small gasp, but a gasp nevertheless, and unclasped the belt she often wore with slacks. Slowly he pulled it from the loops and then unbuttoned the pants themselves. He was able to draw them down to her hips, and roll them past without having to stand her up. The rest was easy, as he slid the pants down to her ankles, and then past each bare foot. He was able to stay on his knees as he unbuttoned her blouse, ever so slowly, one button at a time, until her chest and black lacy bra were revealed. He touched neither, which almost made her groan, as he slipped the top from her shoulders. Only then did he stand, so he could reach behind to unhook the bra, with he did with familiar expertise. He then slid the lacy thing from her shoulders, barely grazing one nipple as he dropped it to the floor. Both nipples were already extended and hard, which made him smile. Then he bent to one, and began to lick it with his tongue, licking in concentric circles around and around for the longest time – or that was how it felt to Sara, who thought she might pass out – before taking it fully in his mouth and gently sucking. When she reached for his belt buckle, he shook his head no, whispering 'not yet', massaging her other nipple with the fingers of his other hand.

Then he reached below and smiled, a slow, sly smile.

"You're very wet young lady. I think you may have done this before, or maybe you've just been made for this activity. What do you think?"

"Oh Michael, please," Sara moaned.

"Please what?" he asked her.

"Please let me touch," she replied.

"But how will you know what to do?" he teased, continuing the game.

"My mother always told me I had a vivid imagination," she said as she began to stroke his erect penis.

"Probably not the best time to mention her. She might not approve," he whispered.

"Oh yes she would. She would be jealous, I'm sure," Sara gasped as she slid his pants to the floor, not nearly as gently as he had removed hers.

When she took him in her mouth, he could barely contain himself.

"You better stop, or I won't be able to satisfy you," he panted, surprised he had been able to speak at all.

She obeyed briefly, only to say 'we have all night' with his penis still in her mouth. He only managed to hold back for a few seconds and then exploded.

Sara licked her lips. "Yum," she grinned at him. "I love your taste. It's sweet, with just a little bit of a tang."

They didn't need all night. Within minutes he was hard again, although he whispered that he didn't think he would be able to come. But after he had slid inside her, he wasn't so sure. She grinned a wicked grin, moving her hips around, side to side, and back and forth. Then she opened her mouth and made the oddest sound, one familiar to both of them, as she came. Michael was wrong: he came as soon as she began to moan, whimper really. He lay half on top of her, half on the bed, but didn't try to move since he knew she would object. They stayed like that for quite a while, both of them spent, neither wanting to draw apart.

Finally Sara asked, "Do you think we should get back to the boxes?" Michael howled with laughter, which finally rent them asunder. She got off of his bed and headed for the bathroom. When he heard the shower, he rose to join her. She really intended to pack more boxes. What a woman!

Tingle

She was happily soaping herself when he stepped into the shower stall, singing "I Can't Get No Satisfaction", which made him start to laugh all over again.

"Incorrigible," he said as he grabbed the bar of soap from her.

"You had better wash yourself," she laughed. "I don't trust either one of us if you don't." She did allow him to towel her dry, but when he moved her legs aside she reached down and took the towel from him. "Uh uh," she told him. "I do intend to get more done tonight."

"So do I," he guffawed.

"Shame on you. I don't think we mean the same thing."

"Depends on how late you plan on staying up," he replied without hesitation.

"You have to go to work tomorrow," she reminded him.

"Not a problem," he said, eyes twinkling. "I just hope you'll have accomplished as much here as I will there."

As he headed for the living room, she called after him, "I think we bought some cheddar at the market over the weekend. Crackers would be nice too."

"Bossy," he called back. "Is this what I can expect over the years?"

"You betcha," she said as she buttoned her blouse and walked into the kitchen. What she didn't say aloud was that Jeffrey had often teased her about her voracious appetite. Somehow it didn't seem appropriate.

. . . .

Two days later they had moved almost all of his remaining things over to the condo, and Sara had unboxed them while he was at the library. By then his co-worker, Bobby, was building the book shelves which were all but assembled, lying on the living room floor, couch and comfy chairs pushed back until Michael could help him lift the large unit up and move it into the hallway to attach to the inside wall. When he came home and the two men raised the bookcase and put it in place, Sara almost swooned with pleasure. Had his co-worker not been standing beside Michael, she would have done so with abandon. A man who loved books as much as she, and also relished her pussy: who could ask for more?

She had been so consumed with helping him move, she had forgotten to call the Justice of the Peace in Stone Harbor. After the weekend she called him immediately, finding his number on the internet. He was delighted to hear from her and gave her several dates to choose from, suggesting she let him know when she had booked a place to stay. The one she and Michael both loved had several openings on the dates he had given her. She chose one and then turned to places their friends could stay, deleting the ones Michael hadn't earmarked as possible and calling the ones he had. All but one were booked for their preferred weekend choice, so she called the Justice of the Peace to make sure he would still be available then. They could always choose another weekend, but not the right person to marry them. He was in a meeting, but called her back a half hour later, apologizing for taking so long to return her call – so long? – and booked the weekend in question. He then reminded her that he needed a copy of their vows, so he could plan what he wanted to say to complement them.

"You know each other and I don't know either of you very well, so that would be helpful," he added. She booked the place she had found for their friends as soon as they hung up.

They both thought the weekend in question a perfect choice –the second weekend in September after Labor Day, crisp but not cold, and she promised to email their vows to him. After he had read them, he suggested he call her back with his proposal of the words he would say as well. She thought that was ideal. He also approved the place they had chosen to stay, a one bedroom beachfront condo overlooking the harbor with spectacular views. He actually knew the owner and was sure they would be very comfortable there. His friend said he would bring them breakfast the morning after the ceremony and leave it by the front door. Neither man thought they should have to make their own breakfast the morning after they were married. Before hanging up Sara reminded him they were a 'mixed race' couple.

"Maybe more marriages like yours will help us to begin to understand one another," came his ready response, which of course pleased her. Sara told him they would write their vows over the weekend, and send them to him shortly thereafter. Since the date was a couple of months away, he told them not to hurry. Getting them right was more important then getting them to him early. 'What a decent man' she thought as she hung up. She liked him more each time they spoke.

Sara made herself a fresh cup of decaf and sat down on her couch. Her shoes came off next, as her feet went up on the oak and glass coffee table in front of it, and then she sighed with contentment. Two months didn't seem that long to wait, though she would have preferred their little ceremony could be sooner, but since neither of them was going to change their mind, it didn't actually matter.

. . . .

The following weekend they drove back to the Pine Barrens again. Paul, the Justice of the Peace, had suggested meeting with them when she called to tell him they were coming down to see the condo they had rented on line.

It was in a lovely setting, close enough to walk in to Stone Harbor, but still secluded and private. Their room had its own spa so they could luxuriate in the water totally naked, without having to share with any other guests. If there were any tenants inhabiting the units next to theirs, they hoped they would be quiet ones. They would have more privacy than either of them had imagined. Neither could understand why the place had not already been taken. Maybe someone had cancelled. They would have more privacy than either of them had imagined. The perfection of the condo made them both feel that this marriage was meant to be.

On the drive back to the City they agreed it might be a good idea to call both Lucy and Jevon with the dates, and called the landlord to see if he knew of another rental close by. He did, and called back within minutes to tell them he had reserved a cabin with two bedrooms nearby, though not on the beach, at a very decent price. Michael told her to put the charge on his credit card, which she already had.

When they called Lucy she said she would move some things around, as she already had plans for that weekend, but wouldn't miss their wedding for the world. "OF course I want to come, and I'm sure Jordan will want to come too, if he's invited." Sara said 'yes, of course' immediately, Michael shrugging his agreement. Sara's cell was on speaker. Then they went through the same routine with Jevon, who asked if he could invite Margery. Michael said he had assumed she would come too, and that was that. "Maybe we'll choose the same place in the spring, and the same Justice of the Peace," Jevon said as if that was the most obvious suggestion in the world. Michael had no idea his friend had such serious intentions with the woman he had been living with… for how long? Michael wasn't sure.

He and Sara detoured to an Oyster place on the way home because another tenant in their building had told them it was a must, and it was.

Tingle

When Sara insisted on finding an ice cream parlor for her dessert, Michael was startled. He was full, and couldn't have imagined eating another bite of anything.

Sara laughed. "I always leave room for dessert."

Standing in line Michael noticed a coconut/chocolate flavor and ordered a cone as well, which made Sara laugh out loud. The girl scooping the ice cream looked surprised but knew enough to not question her customers. Michael was also laughing as the two left the ice cream store. The girl shrugged, muttering, "people" but of course they didn't hear her. It wouldn't have mattered to either one of them if they had.

Michael was happily licking the cone he had said he couldn't imagine eating when he whispered to Sara, "How tired do you think you'll be when we get home?"

Without missing a beat Sara replied, "Not to tired for what you have in mind."

He leaned down and kissed her on the forehead. Then they got into the car, Michael behind the wheel. When they arrived at their brownstone, Sara was the first to step inside the condo, already stripping off her sweater and slipping out of her skirt on the way to the bedroom. Michael was not far behind.

They engaged in very little foreplay, a rarity for them, Michael slipping inside quickly and easily. "You're always so wet," he moaned, Sara grinning up at him.

"So I've been told," she quipped, which inspired a light slap to her left hip.

"I can accept Jeffrey told you that since you were married for so long, but nobody else!"

"Of course not," she replied, deadpan.

"Wow," was all he could mutter after he had come, still inside her, still partially erect.

Sara laughed. "What? You want to try it again?"

"You're incorrigible," he said, adding, "You may wear the little guy out so much he won't be able to perform."

"Not a chance," she declared. "And little? Haven't you heard about black men and size?"

At that Michael belly-laughed. "Black men in general aren't the point, though I must admit I've always thought mine was a fairly decent size," he replied, waggling his by now limp member at her. He was lying belly up so she could easily see what he was doing.

"Braggart," she sighed, quite happily. She had never believed she would ever feel this way again, totally sated, after Jeffrey's death. But this she didn't share with her husband-to-be. It was time to stop comparing the two men, at least aloud.

Chapter 11

Michael and Sara had just begun to unpack their suitcase when Jevon pulled into a spot across the street from their condo. They had decided they only needed to bring one bag since it was still quite warm during the day, probably an effect of climate change. At the last minute they had thrown two jackets into the back seat of the car in case the evenings were chilly, but had not actually packed warm pants or many long-sleeved tops. Sara was delighted at their shared piece of luggage though that felt ridiculous; it seemed symbolic of another way they were joining their lives.

"Maybe his GPS isn't working and they couldn't find their cabin," Michael said as he headed to the door. "I'll be right back."

But Sara was right behind him.

Jevon and Margery had already checked in to their cottage, and thought Michael and Sara might want to share a bottle of bubbly, which he was holding in his hand. He added that Lucy ad Jordan weren't far behind. If all six of them indulged, none of them should be too tipsy to enjoy the words the nuptial couple had written to each other to share at the ceremony or the short speech by the Justice of the Peace. Michael in particular thought the man's speech inspiring, and had filed the copy Paul had sent them for approval. Neither he nor Sara had altered a word of it.

Michael found a stack of upside down plastic glasses on a tray atop the dresser, laughing at the idea of drinking from plastic on this propitious occasion, but Jevon waved him off and began to pour as Lucy and Jordan arrived. All six raised their plastic glasses as Jevon toasted, "To the event we've all been anxiously awaiting. A perfect match, all of our friends on both sides of the aisle agree."

"Yum, I love good champagne," Sara murmured as she took her first sip. "And there certainly isn't enough for any of us to become too high to walk over to Paul's office!"

They all sipped happily, excited that Sara and Michael were going to be married in a few hours. Then they decided to stroll in a leisurely manner to the office where they would tie the knot.

"See, all of us are walking in a straight line," Sara quipped.

"Go faster," Jevon suggested, which she did, purposely weaving from side to side. They all laughed.

"We wanted to tell you all something," Margery giggled.

Sara suspected she knew what she was going to say and was delighted. She liked Margery a lot, happy to have a new friend.

"We've found a bigger apartment to share that we can afford, on 17th Street…" she began, Jevon interrupting, "And we're going to get married in the spring. If we approve of this Justice you keep raving about, we'll probably repeat the process right here."

Tingle

The couples began hugging each other, eliciting honking horns from a few of the passing cars. The vacation community was known for its nuptial ceremonies.

"When Sara first called me to ask if I would perform this ceremony, I knew after a few seconds that I would be happy to – I liked her immediately. She was direct and asked very good questions," Paul began.

Michael took her hand and squeezed.

"We are meeting for the second time, which has only strengthened that feeling. I knew when Sara and Michael drove up here to check me out that we were kindred spirits, which always makes my officiating a pleasure. It was as obvious then as it is now how much these two love each other, and that they belong together. I know that there are many who would not approve of this joining, which makes it all the more important and special to me. I've learned over the years that neither race nor religion nor gender matters when it comes to love. This is one of those times. So let us begin," he said and then proceeded to recite the words he had penned a week before. Sarah realized Michael's lips were moving along with those of the man in front of them, which touched her deeply.

"He really loves me," she thought to herself with wonder. "He really does."

When he said, "I do", Michael had tears in his eyes. Sara managed to hold back hers, since she was sure if even one tear fell, more would pour down.

Much to the surprise of both Sara and Michael, when the service was complete and they had exchanged rings, the Justice of the Peace pulled a bottle of Piper Heidsieck champagne out of his small refrigerator and popped the cork; it was one of Sara's favorites. He hadn't even asked what kind of champagne either of them preferred. All seven of them sipped the delicious beverage, and when it was gone, Jevon took the legal papers from Paul, and then the three couples left his office. By the time they hit the sidewalk, they were all giddy, Sara and Margery actually laughing aloud. Then Sara threw her arms around Michael and kissed him loudly on the lips, causing more merriment as well as beeping from passing cars. No one gave them a dirty look. 'Michael must not have been right,' Sara thought with some surprise.

The Water Star Grille, the restaurant they had booked for their wedding repast, was within easy walking distance. When Margery removed her heels, Sara and Lucy followed suit, even though they didn't have far to go.

"I married a hippy," Michael teased with a chuckle, Sara instantly replying, "There are things best kept secret until after the ceremony." Lucy, Margery and Sara ran ahead, the men following at a slower pace. Lucy leaned over to say, "Jeffrey would be pleased for you, Sara. You know that, don't you?" Sara merely shook her head in agreement, not speaking to keep the tears at bay. Margery took her hand, and the women swung them in the air as if they were still teenagers.

Their table was being held and they were quickly ushered there by the maître d'. The water view was even more spectacular than the one from their condo, which was pretty amazing. Sara lifted her eyes and smiled at her husband. Her husband. Michael was now her husband. Her smile broadened, which she hadn't thought possible. "Have a seat Mrs. Boaten," Michael said as he pulled out a chair for her next to his own at the head of the table.

"I love our name," she declared loudly enough for everyone to hear, causing renewed hilarity. Two cold bottles of Piper were already chilling by Michael's chair; he reached over and popped the first cork, reaching for Sara's glass. Their friends all passed theirs forward as well, which he filled as the waiter placed menus before them. Sara thought the seafood dishes all sounded mouth-watering, and chose the crab stuffed lobster tail. Her new husband chose the sirloin, whispering, "I know I should order fish, but I really love sirloin and I know it'll be great here." She told him to eat whatever he wanted; she certainly didn't care. Jevon followed Michael's lead, Margery and Lucy, like Sara, opting for fish.

"We already ordered the dessert," Lucy told everyone at the table. Margery, who was perusing that part of the menu, closed it with a snap, suggesting, "Why don't we just have one of each dessert on the menu and skip dinner", which elicited the loudest groan from Jevon, who said, "I'm not sure she's kidding."

"I'm not sure I am either," she assured everyone with a huge grin. By then the champagne was flowing, a fourth bottle ordered. When the waiter arrived at the table with a bottle of vodka, a specialty of the restaurant, Sara turned to Michael with raised eyebrows.

"I know it's the only booze you drink so I thought we should all try one of their most esteemed brands," he explained. She kissed him with a loud smack again, making everyone laugh. Their table was certainly not quiet, but no one else in the crowded restaurant seemed to mind.

"They just got married," Margery turned in her seat in order to enlighten the other patrons. The room burst into applause, and someone started to sing, 'Ain't No Mountain High Enough' which the entire room was soon singing, including the wait staff and bartenders.

"I didn't think I liked vodka, but I sure was wrong," Jevon sighed with pleasure as he tasted the liquid in the shot glass the waiter had placed before him. "Wow, this stuff's great!"

Nancy Alvarez

Every single person concurred, though Sara, who loved good vodka, 'Kettle One' her favorite, was the only one who held up her glass for a second shot. "It isn't very far to our condo," she murmured, though Michael told those assembled he would happily carry her there if she could no longer perambulate on her own once the meal had been consumed. More hilarity. Jevon and Jordan offered to help, suggesting they form a seat with their joined hands. Jevon even got up to demonstrate. At that point a man at the next table started to sing Stevie Wonder's 'Signed, Sealed and Delivered,' again joined by the rest of the room.

Michael didn't have to carry Sara to their condo but she certainly wasn't able to walk there in a very straight line. He deposited her on the bed, and went into the large, tiled bathroom to take a shower. He was happily soaping himself when the shower door slid open and Sara stepped inside the airy stall. She rubbed up against his back, saying, "Seems a great way to get some soap without stealing the bar from you." Which she then proceeded to do, making him laugh again. They stood under the cascading water grinning broadly at one another. Then he grabbed the bar of soap from her and began to wash her breasts.

"No fair. I really want to get clean, and I'll never be able to do that if you keep doing what you're doing," she complained in mock indignation, hands on her soapy hips.

"Spread your legs," was his only reply.

She obeyed, groaning as his fingers spread her lips and began to massage her clitoris with his agile, brown fingers. "Oh come on!" she added with a rather large sigh.

Gritting her teeth she took the soap back form him, and began to soap his erect dick. "What's good for the goose...."

Tingle

"Are we going to behave like this once we're back home in the city?" he asked in spurts, unable to say the full sentence all at once.

"We better," she replied, dropping the soap to the floor of the shower as she began to kiss him like a woman possessed. She had always felt passionate with Michael, but this, this was something special. Then Michael grabbed her underneath her butt cheeks, and lifted her thighs up around his own. He slid inside without any effort at all, both of them groaning in unison.

"Don't laugh," he ordered, "Or I'll slip right back out."

By then they were moving in rhythm and there was no chance either one of them would laugh. Both were panting, which might have seemed funny if they hadn't been so intent on the task at hand. She came almost immediately, and he followed her only seconds later.

Gently, he lowered her feet back down to the shower floor, and they stood, bodies touching, water cascading over them both.

"I think I could stand this way forever if I wasn't so tipsy," she chuckled. "I really shouldn't have had that second shot of vodka."

"You'd be standing here alone, because I need to lie down," he told her. "And I didn't have any vodka."

As he turned off the water and reached for one of the huge, fluffy towels hanging on the towel rack Sara said, "As I recall, you had rather a large amount of champagne, almost finishing the last bottle by yourself."

"Our friends are a bunch of wimps," he agreed. He followed her back to the bedroom, lying down beside her and again stroking her body from tip to stern.

"You have to be kidding," she teased, reaching down to see if he was again erect. He was. "I thought I was too tired, but... mmm, maybe not," she murmured. And then their hips were rocking in their familiar rhythm until they both came for a second time in the first hour of the first night of their honeymoon.

"I may not ever be able to get up from this bed," Sara sighed, Michael still lying half atop the length of her. He rolled off with a groan.

"That's not what I meant," she said.

"I was going to crush you," he managed to say, his voice just a low growl.

"Think we should go to sleep?" she asked.

Although he wasn't sure she was serious, he replied, "If we can."

But before either of them could smile, both had drifted into the sleep of the dead. They didn't awaken until after 11 the following morning.

When they walked into the dining room of the best breakfast place in town, the rest of the wedding party was already seated at a table by the window. They all clapped as the newly married couple walked towards their table.

"I win," said Lucy's husband.

"For what?" Sara asked as she dropped into the chair he had pulled out for her.

"For guessing when you would emerge from your wedding suite," he replied to the amusement of everyone seated at the table.

Jevon sniffed the air, adding, "Nothing. They must have stayed in the shower for quite awhile," which set them all into peals of laughter all over again.

Michael was grinning from ear to ear, while Sara blushed to the roots of her hair.

Michael said, "We took one together, and then had to take another."

Tingle

"Michael!" Sara complained, though she wasn't really. Everyone was still laughing.

"Do you want a mimosa?" Lucy asked her old friend.

"I should say 'no', but it sounds delicious," Sara replied.

They sat at the table for a couple of hours, and then everybody else began to get antsy because of the long drive ahead of them. They walked the honeymooners back to their condo, and then the rest of them headed for their vehicles.

Closing the door behind him, Michael immediately pulled Sara into his arms. "I'm too full," she protested.

"You can be on top," he laughed, dropping onto the bed and pulling her down. Before she landed, he was already pulling her t-shirt over her head. Both of them were yet again laughing. But when he bent his head to massage her nipples with his tongue through the fabric of her bra, the laughter stopped short. Sara wiggled out of her shorts, still lying on top of him, and then helped him get out of his.

"Wait," he ordered, reaching down to pull off his own shirt. "Skin to skin. Has to be skin to skin."

Sara tried to sit on him right away, but again he said, "Wait," although he was obviously already quite ready. "Let's do this the right way."

"Which is?" she asked.

"Slow. Real slow," he answered.

And they did.

An hour later Sara had orgasmed three times, unheard of even for them, Michael holding off the entire time. Finally he gasped, "Now!" pulling her on top of him again. Sara was no longer too full. He slipped inside without even thinking about it, holding her hips steady and then began to make very slow circles with his own. Sara thought she would pass out, but she didn't. After just a few minutes, he released her hips, and she too began to move.

"Slowly," he gasped again. Of course she complied, though it wasn't easy.

Finally they lay side by side, utterly sated. "We did it totally right," he sighed.

"The love making?" she asked.

"Getting married. Getting married here. Having brunch with our friends, and yes, then this," he replied.

Both of them sighed in unison, and then couldn't hold back their laughter.

And that was how they spent the first day of their marriage. Making love and laughing.

Sara took Michael's hand.

"We are perfect," she declared.

And they were.

Made in the
USA
Lexington, KY